THE GAME OF TROY

A New York Architect is bidden to the mansion of a Texas billionaire. Will he accept a startling proposition? Will he agree to undertake an extraordinary and fantastic assignment?

The Texas tycoon has a sinister reputation. His house is equipped with all manner of cunning devices, including a lake containing plastic sharks and electronic crocodiles.

Does the eccentric Texan know his wife has been having an affair with the architect? Is there a cold and scheming mind at work behind his innocent invitation?

THE
GAME OF TROY

by

JON MANCHIP WHITE

1971
CHATTO & WINDUS
LONDON

Chatto & Windus Ltd
40 William IV Street
London, W.C.2

★

Clarke, Irwin & Co. Ltd
Toronto

ISBN 0 7011 1667 6

Printed in Great Britain by
Ebenezer Baylis & Son Limited
The Trinity Press, Worcester, and London

To
JOHN O. WEST

... sensation of choking and burning.

This is more than a bad dream. This is a nightmare. Too many martinis again last night. And those sleeping tablets are too strong.

Black. Black. Black. *Why's it so black in this room tonight? Can't see anything—not even the blur of the window. Can't even make out the glimmer where the light comes through the vent of the air-conditioning.*

Why don't I feel the weight of the bedclothes or the pressure of the mattress? Why don't I have a pillow? Why do I seem to be sprawled out on a hard surface?

Is it insomnia? Tension? Overwork? Drinking? A bad conscience? Because of what's been happening between Astrid and me? If she'd only been willing to let me speak up right at the very beginning it would all have been different. Completely different.

Actually, I don't think I'm really in bed at all. Not even in my bedroom. Those tablets do have a damned queer effect.

What's that music all the time? Some sort of crazy waltz? And what the devil happened to my pyjamas? Why am I lying here in my shirt and trousers? And why is my mouth so sore, as if someone had punched me? And my ribs, as if someone had kicked them? ...

Up. Get up. Up slowly.

Weak. Very weak. Legs like water. Take it easy. Crawl a couple of feet.

I

Head's full of smoke . . .

Here. Yes. That's it. The wall. Feels the right texture.

Grope my way along. Gently. Surface is freezing. Use fingertips. Keep body away.

Ah! At last!

The button. Because the main lights are out doesn't mean the guide lights will be out as well. Independent systems. I'll press this button and a guide light will come on. Green or red. A blob of colour in this miserable tomb. No wonder the sweat's running down my ribs. Seems to be getting blacker and blacker. Like being buried alive.

Soon fix that . . .

Press.

Hello? What's up?

Press. Press.

Curious.

Press. Press. Press.

Why's there no light?

Well!

Well! . . .

All just part of it, I suppose . . .

Head starting to spin again. Ringing in my ears.

Ah, that choking sensation . . . burning . . . smothering . . . smothering and burning . . .

YOU know, I thought we'd covered our tracks pretty well, Astrid and me. I thought we'd avoided careless mistakes.

It sounds sordid when I talk about it in this way. It sounds like any other furtive little adultery. It wasn't like that at all. If we were secretive about it, it was because she was determined to spare Gabriel pain. It's true she was scared of him. He was unpredictable. They still have a code about that kind of thing down here in Texas. But there was more to their relationship than that. It wasn't an ordinary relationship because Gabriel wasn't an ordinary man. But if she didn't love him she had a very real affection for him. They'd been married nearly ten years and he'd never treated her in any way that could be described as mean or unpleasant. The legend said he was a great kidder, a great practical joker—which was why it was surprising to find him married to a woman like that.

Until I came along she'd been completely faithful to him. This was certainly the first love affair she'd ever had. Her gentleness and shyness—not feminine qualities usually encountered in the high-spirited state of Texas—were what attracted me to her in the first place. She was standing on the fringe of a noisy party. I remember the nervous little gesture with which the tall, fair, slender girl in the pale blue dress tossed the tress of white-blonde

3

hair out of her eyes as I went across to speak to her. I remember her soft breathless laugh when I told her I was a stranger to Texas too. I said we looked like Babes in the Wood. She laughed because, as she told me with a little stammer, she *was* a Texan—though not, I could see, the usual type of female Texan—strong, confident, extrovert. I was being a bit patronizing, taking pity on her like that. I wondered why her husband wasn't at the party. I didn't know then that he never attended parties, but spent all his free time pottering about his huge place at El Pardo. In any case he was thirteen or fourteen years older than she was, and didn't have much time or energy left over from his responsibilities as head of Sarrazin Resources. I didn't invite her out to dinner after the party. I was sure she'd refuse, and as I was eager to see her again I wanted to avoid a false step.

I ought to say right away that I'm not any kind of Don Juan or professional seducer. In fact I'm a little like Gabriel, in that the assurance of my conversation and bearing lead people to assume that I'm equally assured underneath. That's not so. But at least my air of assurance, like his, is based on the fact that in my own particular field I do happen to know exactly what I'm talking about. If that sounds bumptious, I assure you it's true. Not many modern architects have mastered their craft as thoroughly as I have. In New York, Pittsburgh, Chicago, St. Louis, New Orleans, Toronto, Anchorage, San Francisco, Houston, Dallas, San Antonio, El Paso— even Rio, Buenos Aires, Hobart, Wellington—you can see the buildings that I've designed which prove it.

On the other hand, most of my energies up to that first

evening had been devoted to my profession. There hadn't been much time to spare for anything else. My personal life had been pretty spartan. I'd built myself two fine houses. I liked to buy fast and expensive European cars and drive them in the way they were meant to be driven. But aside from a few college friends I hadn't developed any profound relationships. My relationships with women were superficial. I kept them that way. I was always up to my ears in commissions, conferences, schedules, always working early and late. I fought shy of entanglements that might encroach on my professional activities. I was very jealous of my time. I doled it out grudgingly. As an Easterner, largely employed during the past three years in Houston, Dallas and San Antonio, I'd recently become even more of a slave to my office and drawing board. Socially, I'd always been rather a fish out of water. So I turned the situation to my advantage and retreated further into my shell.

This explained why, when I finally encountered Astrid at Patti Danziger's party, I went so wild. Wild, that is, for a normally highly controlled man. Actually, I'd almost given up going to parties. Of course, they're a good way of making contact with would-be clients. But I had too many clients already. In actual fact I was reluctant to take on any new assignments. This was an enviable position for a thirty-three-year-old architect—but thanks largely to Texas I *was* a very enviable young architect. Naturally, there was a price to pay. I worked sixteen hours a day and wound up by presenting myself with a small but definite drinking problem. As a matter of fact, I felt as guilty about not working this evening as

I felt about the number of martinis I was drinking. I'd
only come along to Mrs. Danziger's party because I'd
just completed for her the house we were standing in—
though 'oriental palace' might be a better description.
And after all, she *was* Mrs. Ralph Danziger. I wasn't so
busy I was keen to indulge in the social and professional
suicide that turning down her invitation would entail.

I won't say it was a case of love at first sight. Let's just
say that there was an overwhelming immediate attraction.
I'm not an authority on these things, but some people
seem to know right away that someone they're introduced
to is destined to have a special meaning for them. That's
what Astrid and I felt, there in that sumptuous Arabian
Nights drawing-room that I'd designed. Anyone looking
at us would have thought he was looking at two tongue-
tied people without much to say to one another. We
stood there shuffling our feet and twirling our martini
glasses. In reality we'd exchanged what a French writer
called *le regard rouge*, the secret glance of a man and a
woman who know they desire each other.

Three days later she came along with Donna Vorbeck
to my office in the Fargeau Building in downtown
Houston. Donna wanted to consult me about some addi-
tional landscaping she wanted at the house I'd built for
her and her husband (the subject of a special number of
the *Architectural Journal* last Easter). Astrid, it turned out,
was Donna's cousin. As a rule I'd have thrown the job
to Ed Edmondson, the expert in Westport who usually
does my landscaping for me. Besides, Donna was tiresome
—silly and talkative. She ran an art gallery in Dallas
specializing in far-out sculpture. She only ran it as a side-

line, as her husband was a vice-president of Sarrazin Resources. She scarcely needed the income. Still, though I didn't like her, this time I took the job myself. I intended to see as much as I could of her beautiful and timid cousin.

From there on it was easy. We met three or four times when I went to Donna's to make notes and measurements. Soon I knew her well enough to enquire casually whether she'd be going to the first night of a play at the Alley Theatre, a concert by the Houston Symphony, or the opening of an art exhibit. Five times out of six she'd find a way of turning up, and we'd be able to have a drink and exchange a few words. Gabriel never went to these cultural affairs.

For two people as predisposed towards each other as we were it wasn't absolutely necessary for us to have a great deal in common. But we did. She'd majored in art and history at Austin, then spent a year in Paris and eighteen months in Switzerland. It was obvious that Gabriel, considerate though he was in other respects, had starved her mentally by denying her any participation in his own work and interests. Perhaps it didn't occur to him that she might get bored, or might find the operations of his engineering and aircraft industries interesting. Certainly she was quickly absorbed by the theory and practice of architecture. I gave her architectural books and magazines to take home to El Pardo. There was also something else. We laughed a lot. Her sense of humour took some time to emerge. It didn't surface all at once. But when I finally reached it, I found it abundant and delightful.

If he neglected her to some extent, Gabriel wasn't stuffy or Victorian. He didn't act as if he believed that a

7

woman's place was in the home. She came and went as she liked, without giving more than the token explanations customary in apparently happy marriages. Altogether, from the little she told me, I was quite unable to credit the stories I'd heard about him being devious and vindictive. I put them down to gossip. I didn't even take it seriously when Axel Johnson, an architect whom I respect, happened to mention that Gabriel had effectively driven him clean out of Texas when Axel had sent in a bill for some work on a Sarrazin Resources plant with what Gabriel thought was impertinent haste. He said Gabriel pursued him with extraordinary violence. I attributed all this to Axel's well-known excitability and tendency to exaggerate.

If we'd been reasonably discreet, we could have had the run of the fabled kingdom of East Texas for as long as we wished. If, that is, we'd wanted to remain just-good-friends. But we didn't. It rapidly became clear that we wanted to progress far beyond that tepid condition. Her elder sister, Beatrice, was married to a California real-estate man and had a home on the Pacific coast a few miles beyond Oxnard, north of Ventura. One of the two houses to which I liked to return between bouts of activity was in Beverly Hills. I'd torn down a mock-Mexican horror on Whittier Drive to create room for it. It was private and secluded. The journey from Oxnard through Malibu and along Sunset Boulevard to Whittier Drive takes a woman driver forty-one minutes. We first fell into bed together on September 13th. We had met at the redoubtable Mrs. D's party on June 28th.

The appetite grows by what it feeds on. These *cinq-à-*

sept meetings were insufficient. Twice, therefore, she went on 'skiing vacations' to Oregon—only the closest she came to Oregon was Whittier Drive. Her sister had a Texan sense of morality, so we thought it kinder not to tell her what was going on. She used to run her red Porsche (like me, she had a taste for European cars) into the garage. Her skis were never unstrapped from the roof-rack. Once we spent a whole week together and never left the house. It was an obsession, a *folie à deux*. Parting from her was a small death. When you remember that she was a Texan, and had been brought up as strictly as her sister, you'll understand that to behave in the way she did she must have been swept right away from her emotional moorings. So was I.

As I said, I was sure we'd covered our tracks. Los Angeles is an enormous and anonymous city. Dallas was fourteen hundred miles away. She was in California on a routine family visit. Every other night she called Gabriel as if she was calling from Oxnard. There was absolutely no reason for him to suspect that she was having an affair with another man. True, a curious thing happened during her second stay with me. I came downstairs late one afternoon to put through a call to my New York office and found that a window was unlatched and a thief had sneaked in. A wooden kachina doll had been knocked to the carpet and trodden on. A portable television-set on a side-table was missing. Nothing else. I suspected the Spanish-American gardener. He had previously stolen a couple of power-tools from the outside workshop. I decided to say nothing because it was all so trivial, and forgot about it.

My house in New York was in the upper seventies, near the park. From the outside it was a dignified old brownstone, but I'd gutted and remodelled the entire interior on unorthodox lines. Astrid was in the habit of flying to New York every October or November to visit the stores. Although Nieman Marcus has everything, even Big D isn't New York, and when we were still in Los Angeles we'd made detailed plans to meet back East two months later. She wasn't happy about it, but she was in love with me. Again and again I'd urged her to marry me. She soothed me, amused me, satisfied me. She'd even managed to make some headway with the drinking problem I mentioned. But she couldn't make up her mind to leave Gabriel. She shrank from hurting him. She also seemed to have some kind of a frightening picture in her mind of the moment when she'd have to explain things to him.

We saw each other five or six times in the interval, always in the company of other people. We exchanged the purest banalities and didn't betray our feelings by as much as a glance across a dinner-table. She hated all this deception, and I'd see her mouth quiver as she raised her glass, carefully avoiding my eyes. I'd see her fingers tap the cloth, frail and pale beneath the Columbian emeralds or South West African diamonds Gabriel constantly gave her. Not to be outdone, I'd gone to Arpels and Van Cleef and bought her a magnificent sapphire, the colour of the first dress I'd seen her in. I gave it to her at La Guardia just before she boarded her plane. She could always explain it away—if Gabriel even noticed it—by saying she'd happened to see it and couldn't resist it.

We were scrupulously careful during that marvellous

week, when the trees in the park were turning a tender gold. We kept the drapes across the windows and came and left by the rear entrance. We stayed in as much as possible during the daytime. When we went out at night we frequented out-of-the-way bars and restaurants. At first, as in Los Angeles, she was restrained and on edge, as if she couldn't shake off the effects of whatever it was that worried her at home. But after a few hours she relaxed. She made love with a frenzy that at first disconcerted me in such a quiet woman. I knew there must be a reason for it: but at the time I simply accepted it with pleasure.

I suppose we did behave now and again like the pair of happy children we were. Some of our trips abroad were probably injudicious, at that. The one to the Met, to hear *Tosca*, or the one to the Museum of Modern Art. My mood was so exalted I was taken completely by surprise when she told me she had a feeling we were being followed. She first said it at the Frick Collection, only a ten-minute walk from my house and where we went one morning. She said it again at Marta's, down in the Village, where I'd booked a table that same evening under another name. Each time I only laughed and put an arm around her. But she couldn't get rid of the impulse to look over her shoulder, so afterwards we stayed indoors and rustled up our meals ourselves.

. . . didn't feel so sick I could think this thing out.

. . . keeps coming and going in waves.

. . . stop taking those sleeping pills.

Nightmare seems worse. Or too many martinis? It's the darkness makes it so bad.

That damned music! If you can call it music. A lot of noise and distortion. One-two-three. One-two-three. One-two-three. One-two-three.

So what's the next step?

If the lights have failed? . . . What? . . . Wait!

Alarm! Buzzer! Independent system. Place bristles with safety-features. Made sure of that!

Now. Visualize those drawings. Stared at them often enough. About ten feet? Eleven feet?

Legs like rubber. Certainly could do with a nice cool . . .

Blast!

Slipped. Lost balance. Bumped wall.

Cold. Hard. Fingers sliding.

Where is it?

Where is it?

Now don't get excited. What's the big rush?

There. That's it! Faint recess of panel. Square outline of button.

Hand's coated with sweat. Feel it dribbling down my wrist.

Bloody dream hasn't got the better of me. All I've got to do is push this alarm—and goodbye dream! *Whole place'll rock like a hive of bees. Dozen alarm-bells'll start clanging.*

Here goes!

Press.

Just listen to . . . !

Well?

THE GAME OF TROY

Where's the ringing?
Press.
Where is it?
Press. Press. Press.
Press. *Nothing.* Press. *Nothing.*
PRESS.

IT was during the long wet spell in March that I got the call from Gabriel Sarrazin.

It came through about three-thirty in the afternoon. The rain was pelting down. It was so dark the lights in the office were on. I was standing at the window watching the cars ploughing through the deluge created by the clogged gutters in South Main Street. There was no point in returning to my rented house in River Oaks while the downpour kept up. I'd work late. I'd send down to the coffee-shop for coffee and sandwiches. I'd sleep on the couch in the inner office.

Then my secretary came on the line.

'A call for you, sir. From Dallas.'

She was flustered. She wouldn't have put it through unless it was important. I'd told her not to disturb me.

The name of Dallas had an emotive effect on me because of Astrid. But she'd never called me at the office. I expected Evie to say that the call was from one of the hundred people I worked with there—contractors, surveyors, suppliers and so on. Her next words shook me.

'Mr. Gabriel Sarrazin, sir.'

For a second I thought she said '*Mrs*. Gabriel Sarrazin.' I'd never even met Sarrazin, let alone talked to him. As I picked up the phone it crossed my mind that Evie might be flustered because she knew (did the whole office know?) about Astrid and me. Then I realized she was excited because the great and legendary Gabriel Sarrazin was on the line in person.

I held the phone a little more tightly.

'Mr. Sarrazın? What can I do for you?'

I heard him say something about just getting back from a meeting in Amarillo. Then he added:

'I think it's about time we had a talk.'

'Oh? What about?'

I'm not sure there wasn't a trace of uncertainty in my tone. This was the voice of the man whose wife I'd been sleeping with. It sounded vaguely familiar. After a moment, with a shock, I realized that it reminded me of Astrid's — light, charming, polite. The Texas accent was slightly more marked, and there was a definite hint of a drawl. Of course, he didn't indulge in 'howdys' and 'you-alls' and that sort of thing. Nevertheless the basic trait of the Texan was still there, and I'd have been wiser to have taken more heed of it.

He greeted me by name and said that I'd been recommended to him by mutual friends. He complimented me on my work. Evidently he'd been checking up on my performance as an architect, for he went on to say how impressed he'd been by five or six projects of mine in and around Dallas, Houston, and San Antonio. It was obvious that he'd actually taken the trouble to go and view them.

I quickly realized I wasn't going to be required to discuss Astrid. The agreeable flow of his words was a clear indication that the poor chap hadn't even remotely suspected what was happening. He was asking:

'How'd you like to take on a job for me?'

'A job?'

A job for Sarrazin could signify a factory, a major installation, a big block of offices. Could I help it if my mouth started to water?

'Here at El Pardo?' he said.

There was no point in pretending I hadn't heard about the wonders of El Pardo. The house and the surrounding ranch occupied about a third of Otero County. I tried to sound like an informed and intelligent stranger.

'Oh yes? At El Pardo?'

'A very big job. Very. In fact, unique. It'll appeal to you enormously. It's a very great challenge and a very great opportunity.'

'Oh? Exactly what sort of job is it?'

'Why not come down to El Pardo so we can talk about it?'

'To El Pardo?'

'Why not stay a few days? You'd like it. It's a show-piece. A fun place. I love getting people down here and showing them the sights. Especially someone like you, who'll appreciate it. Mrs. Sarrazin and I would be delighted to entertain such a distinguished guest.'

I'd been thinking.

'Mr. Sarrazin, I appreciate your calling me this way. But I'm afraid at the moment I'm pretty overloaded. I hate to turn down what sounds like a very fascinating job, but at present I'm absolutely swamped.'

'Believe me, I'm not in the least surprised. A man of your ability and reputation is bound to be in terrific demand. I ought to have got in touch with you sooner. A lot sooner. But won't you at least think it over for a while?'

'Think it over?'

'Please?'

'Well . . .'

'People say a lot of hard things about me, but I've never heard them say I'm not a generous employer. I assure you you'll find the job rewarding financially as well as professionally.'

I hesitated.

'What . . . what did you say about it being . . . unique?'

He laughed. 'Never mind! Just you come on down here and see! What about it? Could you come tomorrow?'

'Tomorrow?'

'Yes.'

'I'm afraid . . .'

'Then what about next week-end?'

'I can't possibly get away from Houston before . . .'

'I can make it very simple. I'll send a plane.'

'Mr. Sarrazin . . .'

I'd made up my mind to turn him down as soon as the job was mentioned. But he sounded so eager and friendly I was finding it hard to refuse him. I was still under the illusion that Astrid and I had handled everything prudently.

His light, pleasant voice came pouring on down the phone.

'Now don't you go turning me down. Give me a chance to explain this thing. After all, it could put a hundred or a hundred and twenty thousand dollars in your pocket.'

He heard me catch my breath.

'Yes,' he said, 'it's that big. Or should I say – that *wild*?'

'Wild?'

He'd certainly gripped my imagination.

'Look,' he urged. 'Why not let the idea simmer for a while? I'm sure if you brood about it you'll find a way of rearranging your plans.' Again I heard the ingratiating little laugh. 'If not, damn it, throw something out! Why don't I give you a call in the morning? At ten-thirty, say?'

It was my turn to laugh. His charm was getting through to me. I'd already half-forgotten he was Astrid's husband.

'That's just about eighteen hours,' I protested. 'You obviously like people to make up their minds in a hurry?'

'Certainly!'

'Still, whether you call me tomorrow or a week tomorrow, the answer's bound to be the same. For one thing, I'm due to start work on a big new house that some people called Cunningham . . .'

'Cunningham? Jack and Margie Cunningham?'

'That's right.'

'Well, I don't see Jack and Margie too often, but they happen to be very old friends of mine. Jack's closely tied up with one of my companies, as a matter of fact. I think I can manage to persuade him to stay in his old home for a while, while you're engaged on this little enterprise for me.'

'Mr. Sarrazin, perhaps I didn't make it quite clear—'

'Why don't you call me Gabriel? Now you go and sleep on it, there's a good chap. Don't rush into a refusal. That's always a mistake. I'll call you at ten-thirty tomorrow. All right?'

He hung up. I could see where he got his reputation as a brisk negotiator.

I was standing with the phone in my hand when Evie burst into the room without knocking. She was well over forty, but she was practically running. Her big bosom was heaving with excitement. Her heavily made-up eyes were brimming with reproach.

'Oh sir! Mr. Gabriel Sarrazin! You can't turn him down! You simply can't!'

We had some wealthy and prestigious clients here in Texas, but none it seemed with the money and glamour of Gabriel Sarrazin.

I smiled into the gummy depths of Evie's mascara.

'I'm flattered, Evie. But I don't think we'll be taking up Mr. Sarrazin's kind offer.'

The big blue eyelids fluttered with dismay. Evie, a native-born Bostonian whom I'd brought with me to Texas, was a tremendous snob. Perhaps she'd already been cherishing visions of week-ends at El Pardo?

'Oh sir! . . .'

'If you'll fetch your notebook,' I said firmly, 'there are several letters I'd like to dictate . . .'

Three days later I was on the road to Dallas.

It was still raining hard. I'd declined Gabriel's repeated offers to ferry me down there in one of his planes and was driving the Maserati I'd imported from Modena six weeks

19

before. This was partly because I didn't want to be indebted to him, and partly because I always found it soothing to get off by myself in a fast car and drive along those magnificent Texas highways through that marvellous Texas landscape. I did a lot of my thinking and planning on those trips.

So there I was between Houston and Dallas with the spray pluming up beneath my tyres. The broad green expanse of the Texas ranches went rolling by. I was warm, I was relaxed – and I was exasperated. Why had I given in? Why was I on my way to El Pardo? If it was embarrassing to talk to Gabriel on the phone, wouldn't it be a hundred times more embarrassing to talk to him face to face? . . .

The reasons for my decision were complicated. There was no doubt that Gabriel had succeeded in generating an interest in his mysterious proposal. On the other hand, there was my instinct to stay clear of him and his ranch. By going there I might accidentally stir up trouble for Astrid. Nor did I want her to think I'd been cultivating her for an ulterior motive. However, since the initiative had come from Gabriel I didn't feel too badly about it.

It wasn't the prospect of a succulent commission that had snared me, although an operation like mine requires constant injections of cash. It wasn't greed for money. It was greed for reputation, greed to excel. Texas had been good to me in this respect. When I first flew down there four years ago to carry out what looked like a quick but lucrative little job, I had the lofty attitude to Texas of the typical New Yorker. My friends made the usual snooty remarks when I told them I'd accepted a small official undertaking in the state capital. I'd never been to Texas in my life. At first I couldn't adjust to those exuberant and outward-going people. Moreover, in spite of the large-scale constructions to my credit, I was disturbed by the swaggering and outrageous demands that Texans made on their architects. I began by being very condescending about them. I sent witty and superior messages back home to the suave citizens of Manhattan.

The truth is, I was too Eastern, too buttoned up. Texas shook me to the depths of my competent and complacent soul. The first big assignment I accepted there was to build a house for Felix Stump near Corsicana. Like most Texas oilmen, he had a mania for big-game hunting. On one of his trips he'd visited Nepaul and Bhutan and been struck by the rulers' palaces. So he instructed me to build his house (it cost nearly a quarter of a million dollars) in Nepalese style. To begin with I treated the whole thing as a joke. Then I became engrossed. Finally I had to admit that I'd never had so much sheer fun with anything I'd built in my whole life.

My second job was similar. Pete Uys had also hunted in India. He'd been impressed by the imperial splendours of Sir Edwin Lutyens's New Delhi. At enormous expense I erected at Ozona a florid purple pile that would have looked more in place on the burnt plains of Bengal than in the soft pastures of Texas. It was a feat of pure bravura, a crazy gloss on the work of the great Englishman. But I had to admit I'd enjoyed it enormously.

By the time Richeson Smith and Mrs. Bonnie Huddleston came along I was more or less broken in. For the former, who'd recently married a girl thirty years younger than he was, from one of the old Mexican dynasties of Laredo, I built a miniature version of the Alhambra. For Bonnie, who was mad about mirrors, I built a mansion that was partly a Persian seraglio and partly the palace of Versailles. As for Patti Danziger, I had no difficulty in meeting her request for a home that would embody water, water, and more water. Havelock Ellis, Simone de Beauvoir, Pierre de Mandiargues and other students of Undinism could have devoted an entire chapter to Patti Danziger's fountains and waterfalls, some of them soaring forty feet high and lit by sealed-in spotlights that changed colour. The principal feature was an indoor pool in the main bedroom, large enough for the Ladies of the Lake to have ferried King Arthur away to Avalon.

Texas liberated me. It freed in me some buried spring of extravagance. In turn it reacted on my buildings elsewhere and made them more striking and intriguing than they would have been otherwise. After four years in that enchanted land, crackling with energy, where there is a grand sparkle in the air, I was ready for anything. No architectural extravagance of any kind was too fantastic to envisage—not to someone who'd reproduced New Delhi, Versailles, Granada, Katmandu and Shangri-La. So when the summons came from Sarrazin, the king of them all, I was already prepared for it, unconsciously lusting for it. What monstrosity or fantastic novelty might he ask me to dream up for him?...

Needless to say, there was more to my change of intention than just the spur to my professional curiosity. There was a complex of personal reasons. I tried to isolate and examine them as the well-bred growl of the engine carried me through the deluge at what my Italian odometer told me was between a hundred and seventy and a hundred and eighty kilometres an hour. For one thing, Astrid and I hadn't been alone together since I'd put her on the plane at La Guardia in late October. Three months and nine days ago. We'd met twice, in company, on neutral ground, and exchanged nothing more than a few polite inanities. I was starving for her. It hadn't been so bad up to the New Year, when I was still basking in the memories of Los Angeles and New York. There had to be a period of separation and recuperation. Like her, I was drained, exhausted, and bruised. But then, in January, my mood began to change and sharpen. My body started to shiver with hunger. I thought of her so incessantly, wanted her so much and was working so hard that I began to sleep badly. That's when I started taking those phenobarbitone pills. I couldn't resist this chance Gabriel had suddenly given me of being close to her.

The irony of poor Gabriel's situation wasn't lost on me. Inviting me right into his house! A man who wasn't just engaged in making love to his wife, but was intent on taking her away and marrying her. Actually, I was troubled about her. When I saw her at Harry Mac-Master's place just before Christmas, and at Wayne Lewkowski's just after it, I thought she seemed listless and unresponsive. As I drove I kept seeing her strained, pale face in front of me. It wasn't that she'd fallen out of love with me—I was sure of that. But why, oh why, wouldn't she marry me? . . .

Did I nurse some idea that by going to El Pardo I might

persuade her to run away with me then and there? Was I heading for some Texas-type showdown with Sarrazin? Perhaps my cool Eastern temperament had been more infected by Southern romanticism than I realized. And if a showdown was in the cards, wouldn't I have been wise to bring someone along to back me up? For a moment I wished the rugged frame of Wendell Barratt, my technical assistant, who'd been nominated for the Heisman Trophy as a tight end, was wedged in the passenger seat beside me. And for a fleeting second it even crossed my mind that perhaps I ought to have brought something to protect myself with—a thought that had never previously occurred to me in the whole of my adult life. I pushed it aside as melodramatic and puerile.

What was Gabriel like? The closer the wet wheels took me to El Pardo, the more curious I became. He didn't like being photographed for the newspapers, that much everyone knew. Not that you can tell much about a man from a photograph, anyway. Was he five feet tall or seven feet tall? Was his hair black or blond or brown? Was his handshake limp or was it the bone-fracturing clasp of the native-born Texan?

All I had to go on was his voice. It sounded civilized and engaging. So why had I been blowing up his image into the likeness of a fire-breathing monster? Oddly enough (again I felt a pang of shame) we'd probably get on very well together . . . poor devil.

Yet I didn't deceive myself. I was prepared for something unpleasant. Sarrazin carried plenty of muscle. He could run me clear out of Texas, as he was supposed to have done with Axel Johnson. Tales of Texan revengefulness aren't fairy stories. Texas is the last stronghold of the vendetta. I seemed to remember hearing at some dinner-table or other that Sarrazin's grandfather—or could it have been his actual father?—had been mixed up in one of the most notorious of the Texas feuds, a private war that went on for nearly ten years and reduced a sizeable chunk of the great raw State to a shambles.

The long hood of the Maserati split the oncoming torrent like the bows of a yacht. It was teeming down so hard I sensed it must soon lift. There was a silver radiance on the rim of the horizon. I kept my foot down.

Another thirty-five or forty minutes and I'd be seeing Astrid. Believe it or not, I was really and truly looking forward to my visit to El Pardo. Yes—actually *looking forward* to it! . . .

. . .go on crawling on my hands and knees along the bottom of the wall. Bound to stumble on one of them. Planted them there myself, less than ten days ago.

Won't panic. Won't panic. Won't panic.

I posted those tags at intervals where the carpet meets the wall. They're small. Unobtrusive. Nobody could have spotted them and removed them. Not even the agency that controls this dream.

My head's still woozy. The blackness keeps churning in

front of me. Like tar bubbling in a cauldron. Something horrible about dragging myself along like an animal. God almighty, this thirst. And still the soreness round my mouth, round my ribs.

The tags are a width of a finger from the base of the wall. If I brush the heel of my palm along the smooth surface I'll touch one of them. They've got a matted texture, different from the wall's.

All I've got to do is to keep following them. They're at fairly wide intervals, but once I've found the first one finding the rest'll be easy.

Wouldn't be hard to miss one, though. They're only the size of a dime. Better slow up a bit.

That stupid waltz. Hammering. Hammering. Hammering. Hammering.

Where's that tag?

Come on, come on!

Where the hell is it?

Damned blackness. Bloody evil dream.

When am I going to wake up?

When? When? WHEN?

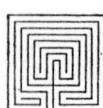

Gabriel's estate began eighty miles south of Dallas. I knew I'd reached it when I began to encounter on each side of the road a tall and shining chain-link fence, made of more solid and expensive materials than the usual run of rusty barbed-wire. The Maserati ran on beside the shimmering silvery barrier for over thirty miles.

The entrance was a turning off the highway on to a wide dirt track. A triple cattle-grid covered the opening and the entrance was spanned by a gleaming steel archway surmounted by the ranch brand and the words *El Pardo* in modern lettering.

I swung the car off the highway and across the cattle-grid. Obviously it would take an age to cross Gabriel's land and reach his house. The land was flat but the grass was plump and green. Neither pains nor money had been spared to irrigate it. The whole huge plain was seamed with a concourse of neatly-engineered canals. There were pumps and water-tanks round which the cattle were clustered thickly. The entire landscape was dotted with them. I saw Herefords, Guernseys, Friesians, Jerseys and a bulky breed of a flawless cream-white colour that I couldn't identify. Screened by trees, the houses of the ranch-hands stood on either side of the dirt road.

The rain had stopped. There was a brilliant rift of lemon yellow in the gunmetal sky ahead. The weather was clearing. There would be one of those spectacular sunsets I enjoyed so much – a Texas fruit-salad of pinks and purples, mauves and lavenders, scarlets and saffrons. I drove faster, feeling the broad bite of the tyres in the damp dirt of the road.

Ahead of me, through the crescent on the spattered windshield, I could make out a dark line. It was a wide arc of trees. They marched towards me down a rise like an old-style army advancing *en masse*. The flanks came crowding in like encircling cavalry. In the centre I glimpsed a white rectangle. Then I was among the woods, the pines pressing all around the car like giant grenadiers.

They were pines of the type which smother the whole of north-east Texas from Texarkana to Greenville with a sumptuous pelt. I guessed that the white square in the middle was the roof of the upper portion of El Pardo itself, lurking behind its lance-like rampart of trees. And there, only a few short miles away, Astrid was waiting to meet me.

She was closer than I thought.

Where the verges of the dirt road converged to a dark brown point I made out a bright crimson dot.

I slowed. It was Astrid's Porsche, parked diagonally across the road, door wide open.

I drove past it and pulled to the side and stopped. I switched off the engine. Astrid was already running out from between the trees on the other side of the road. The toes of her high black boots kicked up small scads of sodden dead leaves and pine needles. She was dressed in creased white linen trousers and a short black reefer jacket with brass buttons. Her fair hair was caught back by a cream silk scarf.

My smile of greeting disappeared as soon as I saw her expression. She hurried to the window which I'd started to lower as soon as I'd spotted the Porsche. She was fighting for breath, like a deer with the pack after it in

28

full cry. She shot a glance over her shoulder as if at any second she expected to hear the hounds baying and see them come bounding out of the wood.

'Quick!' She had the key of the car in her hand. '*Quick. Please!*'

'Darling, what the—?'

'Follow the Porsche. I've got to talk to you.'

She darted away from the window towards her own car. She slipped behind the wheel, slammed the door, started up and came lunging by me in one continuous movement. Mystified, I pressed the starter and took off in pursuit. A hundred yards down the road, without any warning, she veered to the left and shot down an inconspicuous side turning. I was caught napping, overshot, and had to reverse. She went on ahead without slowing down.

After about a minute of furious driving I found myself spinning along the raised levee of an enormous lake. We came on it abruptly. It reminded me of a wooded lake in a corner of Europe, in the Black Forest or in the wilds of Scotland. It was extraordinary to stumble on that dark and romantic stretch of water in the middle of a Texas plain. That evening it looked sombre and reedy and forlorn. A band of lemon-coloured sunlight irradiated the distant shore.

The Porsche gave me no time to savour my surroundings. I had to push hard to keep up with it. Leaves and pine needles lay thick on the track and we ran on between the mournful glades and the curving shore with a muffled softness. Then the Porsche's brake lights winked briefly as it swung left over a small stone bridge.

The bridge connected the shore with a little island about an acre in extent. On the middle of the island stood a white belvedere or gazebo. It was constructed to command a wide view of the lake. Astrid drove in behind it where her car would be concealed in the stretch of shadow between the belvedere and the trees. I followed suit

The belvedere was a replica of an eighteenth-century original. It had bulging bow windows and a pair of glass doors flanked by stucco columns. It resembled a rustic folly at the Petit Trianon or Schönbrunn. The white wooden exterior, with its Greek-key patterns around doors and windows, had been allowed to weather to a natural patina. It had an air of disuse. Astrid left her car and jerked open the glass doors and vanished inside. In a moment I saw her motioning through the panes as if beseeching me to hurry.

As soon as I entered she shut the doors and leaned with her back against them. The belvedere was unheated. I regretted the warmth of the car. Then she rushed towards me and we embraced and I forgot all about the chill and the smell of damp and the long drive and the three-month separation.

We sat side by side on a black leather sofa in front of a marble fireplace with an iron bucket piled with logs. The leather was cold and musty. There was a film of dust on the dry surface of the logs.

She was staring at me with big nervous eyes. Her voice shook.

'I'd been waiting for you ... hours ...'

I wrapped my arms around her more tighly. Above the fireplace and nailed on the walls were trophies of skulls crowned by spreading horns with tiny delicate twisted spikes. The skulls were arranged in fancy designs. They looked like a sort of florid celebration of death.

'Why did you come? I couldn't believe it when Gabriel happened to mention it last night.'

'Why? Because he phoned me —'

'Phoned you? Gabriel did?'

'Yes.'

'He called you? But what about?'

'He wants to consult me.'

'Oh?'

'Professionally.'

'Oh!'

'And it was a great chance to see you.'

'What's he up to?'

'How do you mean?'

'I know Gabriel!'

'What would he be up to?' A sudden thought struck me. 'Or did you talk to him?'

'Why should I do that?'

'Because you wanted to see me as badly as I wanted to see you. Did you suggest I might do some sort of a job down here?'

'Darling, do you imagine I'd have talked about you to Gabriel? Ever?'

'It might have come up quite innocently. Anyway, there's nothing very odd about him getting in touch with me, is there?'

'No?'

'He said he'd heard of me. He'd have been bound to, wouldn't he, sooner or later? He's always needing archi- tects. His companies are putting up plants and factories all the time.'

She was unconvinced. She kept saying she couldn't believe the whole thing had happened in a perfectly ordinary way. She thought there must be some deep dark plot.

I cupped my hands round her face. She didn't want to look at me. She sat with her hands thrust in the pockets of her jacket. Her cheeks were very cold. There was a line between her grey eyes as if, like me, she'd been sleeping badly.

I said softly: 'Astrid . . . listen—'

But all at once she broke out of my arms and stood up. Clumsily she leaned down and clasped her hands round my face. I was astonished to see that tears were spilling out of her eyes. She bent and pushed her mouth with greedy tenderness against mine.

'Astrid!'

She took my hand and pulled me to my feet. Her fingers were shaking.

'We can't stay here. He'll miss us. He'll get suspicious.'

'So what?'

She fumbled a small scrap of a handkerchief out of the pocket of her slacks and scrubbed at her cheeks and eyes.

'He'll see I've been crying.'

'What if he does? What *is* this?'

She balled the damp handkerchief in her palm.

'If only I knew what we could *do*.'

'Do? How do you mean, darling? There's plenty we can do.'

'You don't know him ...'

'Darling, we can do whatever we want. You've only got to make up your mind about marrying me. I'll speak to him at the first possible moment.'

'No!'

'But why not?'

'As I said—you don't know him—'

'But I'll have to, sooner or later.'

'Promise me you won't say anything till I say so.'

'Darling—'

'Promise!'

'I don't—'

'And you've got to promise something else, too—'

'What?'

She stepped closer to me. 'That you'll go away tomorrow.'

'Go away?'

'Leave El Pardo. Tomorrow morning. And whatever it is he says he wants you to do for him, you won't do it.'

'Astrid—!'

'Promise!'

'But what's the harm in at least hearing what he—'

'No! You must get away as quickly as possible. Make some excuse. And you must stay away.'

'Why are you making such a big thing out of all this? I don't under—'

'Stay away! This isn't just the sort of routine affair you could have with another woman. Don't you understand

33

that? I wish I'd never got you into this. Darling, go away and stay away!'

'But, darling, be reasonable. What could he possibly be—'

'I don't know. But there's bound to be *something*!'

She had already turned away from me and was walking quickly towards the door. I shook my head as I followed her. At the door she swung round and thrust her arms round my neck. I held her, embracing her hungrily. Her unhappiness and uncertainty tore my heart. Then she pulled away and opened the glass door. A cold gush of air nipped into the belvedere.

Just behind the door as she tugged it open I saw a squat metal contraption like a miniature computer. It had a kind of console studded with thirty or forty black buttons and a line of red ones. Without thinking and out of pure curiosity I put my hand out towards it. I thought it was some kind of giant hi-fi. My fingers strayed over the red buttons.

'*Don't touch it!*'

I jerked my hand back as if I'd been stung.

She said: 'You'll set off the nightingales or something . . . —'

'Set off the *what*?—'

She lifted a hand through the open doorway in the direction of the lake.

'It's all connected with that.'

'Ah!' I nodded appreciatively at the darkening expanse of water. 'He was lucky to find a stretch of water like that when he came here.'

'Find it? He made it.'

34

'*Made* it?'

'Yes.'

'But it's vast! Like a small sea!'

'That wouldn't worry him. He never does anything by halves.'

'Obviously.' I could just make out what looked like a long line of slipways about a mile away. They were almost invisible against the evening-shadowed woods. 'I suppose it's quite shallow, then?'

'Shallow?' She was impatient to be off. The chill breeze ruffled her hair and she put up a hand to smoothe it down. Her voice was rapid and indifferent. 'I wouldn't call it shallow. It's forty feet deep.'

'Forty *feet*!'

'Yes.' She was hurrying towards the Porsche and spoke without bothering to turn her head.

I started after her, giving a low whistle.

'Forty feet! . . . You're right . . . He doesn't do things by halves! . . .'

I could see Wendell Barratt's big body huddled over the drawing-board as he puzzled out the calculations for a big job like that. I could picture the bulldozers and earth-moving equipment.

She had reached the car and was looking back at me as I came up.

'Let's hurry. He's got some kind of a gadget on the front gate of the ranch. A camera, and some sort of timing device.'

'If it's worrying you that much, I can always say I stopped to admire the view, can't I? But why don't we simply tell the truth? Why not tell him you came to meet me? You're going to be my hostess, aren't you?'

She nodded, managing to smile.

'And he told you I was coming, didn't he?'

Another nod.

I squeezed her hand. 'Well, then!'

She shook her head. 'You don't understand.' She stood there in the dusk and gave me a curiously intent look.

'Darling, I'm not behaving this way because I don't . . . If I could . . .'

She gripped my arm and stood on tiptoes to give me a swift darting kiss. Before doing so she glanced round quickly as if the nearby pine trees might be full of eyes. Her lips were dry and hot.

Then with the same furtive grace of the hunted animal she'd shown when we met she slid behind the wheel of the Porsche. She looked up out of the window and spoke in a rapid voice.

'You drive on ahead, darling. Just go back round the lake to the main drive again and turn left.'

'What about you?'

'I'll go the other way and come in by a different road. I told them at the house I'd be visiting the wife of one of the foremen. I'll drive down there now. She came back from the hospital yesterday.'

I shrugged and nodded. It all seemed rather melo-dramatic.

She went on: 'I won't reach the house until at least half-an-hour after you do.'

She drove off rapidly without switching on her lights. The car was swallowed up by the gathering darkness as soon as it crossed the small stone bridge.

I got into the Maserati and drove in a leisurely way in the direction she told me. No need to hurry now. I put the window down and enjoyed the fresh damp air. The whole unexpected scene had surprised and slightly unnerved me. I put on my headlights, thinking about the summerhouse as I drove. Across the lake, above the shrouded purple of the pines, a last thin band of light shone a clear topaz yellow as the night dropped down.

I glanced at the inky water. I didn't know it, but to-morrow morning I was due to return there. I'd be given a special tour of the ranch, the lake, the summerhouse and a score of other features of the estate. My guide would be none other than their owner and my prospective employer himself. The summerhouse, like everything else, would turn out to be highly original and ingenious. The console I'd almost touched would prove to be fitted with a battery of special devices, all of them connected with the lake. As I'd been warned, one button set off recordings of artificial nightingales, transmitted by amplified micro-phones situated at strategic points. There were buttons that set off owls, nightjars, warblers and various other species of bird noises. Other buttons released swans, mallards, pintails, teals and Muscovy ducks from a col-lection of individual breeding pens. Still other buttons controlled invisible dams and sluices that raised or lowered the level of the water. There were buttons that sent music floating dreamily across the lake, while a whole array of rheostats made possible a fantastic combination of lighting effects. Spotlights were positioned among the trees, along the shore line and right under the surface of the water. There were lights of every size and colour. On summer nights it must have looked like fairyland. There was also a special row of buttons that served a very different purpose. These were the red ones. A touch of one of the red buttons and the mild summer night would be filled not with the warble of nightingales but with the howling of coyotes and jackals. And to make the flesh creep further, another button could send a shoal of horribly realistic plastic crocodiles slithering into the water. These could be steered electronically in any direction and made to creep up on any unsuspecting swimmer or fisherman. Finally, as the *pièce de résistance*, another button unleashed the plastic black fins of a school of sharks. These too were controlled from the panel in the summerhouse. They could be manoeuvred right up to the rim of the shore and made to dance a sinister ballet. Gabriel demonstrated for me. He had a very light and delicate touch on the console.

... horrible feeling my life's got itself back to front. Feel as if I've been picked up by a big ghostly hand. Turned inside out. Like a sock or glove. Split like a herring ...

... Could I be dead? Is that it? Is that what's happening?

... Limbo? ... Hell? ... Or some sort of tunnel? ... Something we've all got to crawl through after we die? ...

Die? ... So confused ... sleepy ... those tablets ... How could I have died? ... All the rain and slush? ... Don't

remember anything like that . . . Surely something of that kind
— loss of control — other car or tree or side of a bridge or a white
face sliding towards you at ninety or a hundred . . . Bloody
smash . . . Agony . . . Surely I'd have remembered that? . . .

. . . Can't pretend any more I don't feel panic . . . Sour taste
. . Sweat on my body smells acid . . .

I've got a sense I'm not alone in this tunnel, or whatever it is.

I've got a definite feeling there's someone else. A few yards
away.

. . . Or could there be more than one? . . . Legion of lost
souls? . . .

ALL the same, I felt a slight flutter in the stomach as I stood on the portico with its soaring pillars and spreading pediment and saw my car being driven into the falling darkness. A burst from the exhaust, a spurt of gravel, and the Maserati rounded the far end of the long white building and disappeared from sight. I felt oddly alone and naked, like someone caught in the middle of a wood with the darkness crashing down.

I turned and walked towards the front door, flanked by two of the servants who had been waiting for me at the foot of the portico. They seemed to materialize out of the air. They wore slacks and red turtleneck sweaters. The leader, who also wore a black blazer with silver buttons, smiled briefly and murmured a polite 'Good evening, sir.' He wore spectacles with smart square black frames. The impression he gave was intelligent and studious. They were young men, all three of them: serious, concentrated, well-barbered, athletic, more like junior executives than servants.

My bags were out of the trunk before I climbed from behind the wheel. I ascended the front steps with my two-man escort. This was an efficient and purposeful household.

The front door swung open at our approach like the gate of an enchanted castle. My glimpse of the belvedere had already prepared me for Gabriel's mania for

gadgeteering. Nothing would be done by hand if it could
be done by means of a photo-electric cell.

I gave the building a brief professional glance before
I went inside. There was hardly any light left in the sky
but it confirmed the glimpse I'd caught as I came up the
drive. The house was grand but not very distinguished, a
copy or a heavily-restored version of one of the ante-
bellum mansions of the Old South. I was disappointed.
I'd imagined the house would correspond to the reputation of its owner. I'd expected it to be one of those weird
Texas follies I'd come to like and of which by now I'd
furnished a good many specimens myself. El Pardo only
succeeded in giving me a feeling of elephantiasis. It didn't
strike me at all as being the 'fun-place' Gabriel described.
But I'd already been wrong about the belvedere, which
also looked perfectly ordinary on the outside and
obviously contained plenty of surprises once you entered
it. Maybe the house was the same. Was Gabriel secretive?

We passed through a huge hallway and up a broad
stairway. Like the summerhouse, the hallway was fes-
tooned with the skulls of dead game. I found that the
suite of rooms which I was to occupy were also laid out
on what might be called an electronic basis. At strategic
points—beside the bed, on consoles and coffee tables—
were miniature remote-control panels with neatly labelled
buttons. Without leaving my bed I could open and draw
the curtains, raise and lower the blinds, operate the radio
and television, slide back the doors of the closets, switch
the lamps on and off and make them dimmer and
brighter. The master of El Pardo seemed to have an
inclination to play the magician.

The bathroom was laid out as lavishly as the bedroom. There were electric razors and safety razors and a choice of hot lather from dispensers or cold lathers in ordinary cans. A regiment of lotions stood on the marble basin beside the gold taps. The bath and the shower were sunken affairs that would have pleased the Emperor Tiberius, their enormous gold fittings massive enough to gladden the heart of Patti Danziger, my Houston client who spent half her life immersed in scented water.

Although I fought against it, I still couldn't prevent myself from feeling tense and uneasy as I put on a fresh shirt and a dark suit and made myself ready to meet my host.

At first sight my fears seemed groundless. It would have been hard to imagine a friendlier reception than the one Gabriel gave me. It didn't seem possible that he could ask me to build anything sinister or monstrous.

He was talking on the phone. As soon as I entered the drawing-room he put down the receiver, picked up a glass and walked across the room with it.

'I expect you can do with this.' He smiled. 'Welcome to El Pardo. I'm afraid you aren't seeing it under very agreeable circumstances.'

I was putting out my hand to take the glass.

'I beg your pardon?'

'The weather. Perfectly foul. You like martinis, I suppose?'

He put the glass in my hand.

'Oh yes,' I said. 'The weather. Horrible!'

'You *do* like martinis?'

'Oh yes! I like martinis!'

'Good. My wife will be down in a minute. She went out after lunch and came back only a few minutes ago. I know how much she's looking forward to meeting you.'

I sipped my drink and said carefully: 'Your wife and I have met before, actually.'

He took my arm and steered me over to a sofa.

'So I gathered, but that was only casually, wasn't it? At the house of some friends?'

He was standing over me, smiling down at me. He'd picked up a half-full glass of what looked like milk from the top of the bar as we walked past it.

'How's the martini?'

'Fine!' I indicated the glass in his hand. 'But aren't you having a drink yourself? Or is that a Brandy Alexander?'

'This? Oh, I don't drink! Never have. I don't smoke either. But don't you get the idea I'm some sort of a puritan. I like to see other people enjoying themselves. Actually, I think I mix martinis rather well, don't you?'

'You mixed this?'

'El Pardo's famous for its man-size martinis . . . You're sure you like them?'

'How do you know how to mix them, if you don't drink them?'

'Ah! I have a great gift for pleasure at second-hand. Does that sound strange?'

'Well, a little unusual, perhaps.'

He laughed. His laugh, like his smile, was attractive. He had charm. His warm brown eyes twinkled continuously. His rather fleshy lips were constantly drawn back from the fine square white teeth. He was rather smaller than I'd imagined, not big for such an important man but broad-shouldered and strong-looking. His complexion was very brown—though whether this was due to what I'd heard about a touch of Mexican ancestry or the effects of outdoor life I didn't know. The main impression he gave was of abundant energy. He liked to stand with his legs apart, thrusting his body squarely towards the person he was talking to. He tended to step close to you, invading your private space, pressuring you. If you were taller than he was, he liked to make you sit down so he could remain standing, making it easier to dominate you. His manner was friendly but relentless. His restless vitality was visible in the way he had of twitching his shoulders, the constant movements of his head and hands, even in the waves of his thick auburn hair that seemed to crackle with electricity. One thing in particular that immediately struck me about him was the unlined appearance of his face. He was ten years older than I was, but we looked the same age. He was dressed informally, in the same red turtleneck sweater and dark blazer as the young man in the driveway. He was putting himself out so strenuously to be agreeable that I don't know where I got the impression from that he might be sly and dangerous.

We were talking in the same desultory way when Astrid came in. She entered the enormous room quickly, still as rushed and flustered as she'd been an hour before. She'd put on a green silk dress and her hair looked freshly combed and slightly damp, as if she'd just hurried out from under the shower. Gabriel went up to her and wrapped an arm around her. He drew her towards me, the picture of fond possessiveness.

I rose politely and shook the hand she held out to me. I gave it a little squeeze but felt no response. Beaming, Gabriel effected the introductions, telling me that now Astrid and I had met properly he was sure we'd get along splendidly. He made her sit down beside me on the sofa. His brown eyes shone happily down at us, as if he was delighted at the cosy spectacle of his wife and his new friend seated so close together. His lips were drawn back in the familiar grin and his slightly snub nose was wrinkled with pleasure.

He gave a start and touched Astrid on the shoulder.

'Forgive me, darling! I was forgetting. You'll have one of my specials, of course? We've plenty of time before dinner.'

He moved smartly to the well-stocked bar on the far side of the room and picked up a silver pitcher. Astrid and I exchanged a quick glance. She looked pale. Her eyes seemed to be begging me to keep quiet and not stir things up. When she was in her husband's presence she was a totally different person from the lively and amusing woman I was in love with.

When Gabriel handed her her drink I smiled at her and said:

'Well, I'm glad to see *you* drink, Mrs. Sarrazin. It's nice to have company.'

She looked up nervously at Gabriel, looming above us, legs straddled, a newly-replenished glass of white liquid grasped firmly in his hand. He smiled down at her fondly.

'Oh well, I've done my best to break her of these nasty habits — though I haven't had much luck, as you can see! . . .'

'Why don't you drink, yourself? Did you have parents who were good Texas Baptists?'

'Oh no, nothing like that! No, I tried drinking once, but it just didn't suit me.'

Astrid had tilted her chin up at Gabriel's reference to her. She took a mouthful of her drink in a way that struck me as quietly defiant. I was rather annoyed to notice that she wasn't wearing the sapphire I'd bought her, only one of Gabriel's gross-looking diamonds. Then the flash of defiance vanished almost as soon as it appeared. She stared down into her lap.

As I made efforts to make conversation I studied the drawing-room. It was ornate and conventional, like the house itself. There was no indication that Astrid had any hand in designing or decorating it. It was impersonal. The only individual touch was a large picture over a buffet near the door at the far end. It was too far away for me to make it out. It looked interesting, and I decided to take a look at it when I had a chance. Otherwise the place was bland and almost barren, though I had no doubt that it was strung with the same invisible spider-webs of electric wiring as all the other rooms in the house. One of the control devices lay on the coffee-table in front of me, beside a chessboard with a set of steamlined chessmen cut out of polished steel. The chessboard wasn't just an ornament. A game was in progress. I hadn't played chess since I left college, but it looked to me as if the opposing sides were locked in a particularly intricate and bitter end-game. Was he playing against himself? Or with one of the young men who waited on him?

I complimented him on what I'd managed to see of his house and ranch. I told him how impressed I'd been by the sight of his rolling acres. I mentioned the fine herds, particularly the white cattle that had been unfamiliar to me.

His eyes lit up. He swayed back from the hips.

'Ah! You noticed my Charollais! It's not exactly surprising you didn't know what they were—very few of my guests do. Still, I doubt very much if there's really much you don't know, is there? Everyone tells me you're a very clever chap and that I'll be very lucky if I can get hold of you!'

He said it without any apparent tinge of irony.

I explained that my grandparents had come from the pastures of Leicestershire to be dairy-farmers in Vermont. When I was a boy my father took me to livestock shows all over New England. This interested Gabriel. Waving his glass of milk (I was pretty certain it was milk now) he launched into an eloquent account of the care and rearing of Charollais. He went into details of their behaviour in their native France and in different parts of America. He talked about lactation and milk yields. He was a fanatic about cattle, as I suppose his Texan ancestors were before him. From childhood I was used to men who were crazy about farming, and at first I listened tolerantly, even with pleasure. Astrid sat with a glazed expression, as though she'd heard this same dialogue a hundred times before. But she began to grow restive and embarrassed when her husband insisted on going into the finer points of breeding. There was one outstanding bull he owned called

47

Leonidas. Its sexual prowess seemed to excite him and cause him tremendous satisfaction. It must have been one of the most potent animals in Texas—in America—to judge from the figures Gabriel reeled off concerning the number of cows it could cover and the number of off-spring it produced. It was currently the most expensive stud-bull in East Texas, pumping out seed in a seething flood. I gathered that Gabriel was fond of riding down to the corrals to watch Leonidas do his stuff, and liked to take parties of visitors down there for the same purpose. I could feel Astrid growing tense on the sofa beside me as the description went on and on and became more and more anatomical. It was certainly rather a strange mono-logue. I looked up into Gabriel's face as he bent over us, sawing away with his glass. I'm moderately fond of milk, but I eyed that glass with distaste. His eyes were bright, his rather prominent lips were wet. There was a filament of spittle at the left-hand side of his mouth as it opened and shut.

I think I was growing a little crimson myself, when we were saved by an interruption. The bespectacled young man who had supervised my arrival was standing in the distant doorway. He waited until there was a fractional lull in Gabriel's discourse. Then he raised his voice, to make sure it reached us, and announced that dinner was ready. He was still wearing his previous outfit of slacks, sweater and blazer. It must have been the El Pardo uniform.

Gabriel looked cross at being forced to terminate his recital of Leonidas' amorous achievements. If I hadn't happened to be actually watching him I wouldn't have

48

witnessed it, but for a second his smooth face was trans-
figured by an oddly devilish look. It was like the stroke
of lightning that fissures a summer landscape and reveals
it in a completely new light. He paused a moment, looking down at the chessboard. All at once he moved a queen
and removed an opposing knight from the board. Then
he stood back and suddenly smiled, motioning us to leave
the sofa and walk ahead of him, side by side, towards the
door. The young man stood aside for us in the easy but
respectful attitude with which he had previously seen to
the disposal of my car and luggage. If he knew that he
had momentarily annoyed his employer, he didn't show
it. Perhaps Gabriel's forked-lightning reaction was too
frequent to be significant?

Before leaving the room I paused briefly to examine the
picture over the buffet. It disconcerted me. Nothing I'd
seen so far in Gabriel's surroundings led me to suppose he
was particularly concerned about the arts. And now I
found myself admiring a modern painting of exceptional
quality. It was unsigned, though I rather thought it must
be by Masson. It was painted very freely, in acid greens
and scarlets with a few small areas of violet and amethyst.
It showed a man and a woman, their bodies bent and
gashed, running with hair streaming and heads strained
back in terror. They wore classical robes, stained, ripped
away to show their sexual organs. They were posed
together on a kind of plinth, as if they were statues, and
enclosed in a room or shrine. They were pursued by a
swarm of winged insects, ants or hornets, that had either
flown into the room from outside or which emanated
from their own suppurating wounds. In a square window

or doorway behind them a volcano was erupting, spitting out great blocks of glowing granite into the sombre sky. On its slopes a building with columns and a pediment was being blanketed by molten lava. Long grass and poppies grew round the foot of the plinth. What was particularly striking was the way in which the man and woman were fused together. They were literally one flesh, joined or hinged into a single scampering figure. The sexual organs were exaggerated, the man's clutching hands fastened on a jutting breast and on a swollen vulva whose gaping interior was furnished with interlocking tines like the inside of a gigantic conch-shell.

I heard Gabriel's voice behind me. He laughed.

'Quaint, isn't it?'

'A very fine painting.'

'Know how I got it?'

'No? How?' I turned round and moved closer to it.

'I was at Ranald McFee's place, up in the Panhandle. He buys a lot of that kind of stuff. It's for investment, though I suppose he's got to have some sort of hobby since his umpteenth wife left him, and he got busted up playing polo at Midland. Anyway, it was on his wall, and as we were eating he saw it'd caught my fancy. I couldn't tell you why, but it had. It wasn't like any of his other pictures, which were mainly hunting and race-horses. He said it'd got sent down from Washington or somewhere by mistake with a regular shipment and he hadn't bothered to send it back. He's got paintings all over his walls, even the lavatories. When he saw the way I kept looking at it he called in a gardener and told him to take it down and fetch it along to the airstrip. He gave it me as a little sweetener to help along the deal we'd been roughing out. I brought it home in the jet and had Larry here—' he put his arm round the shoulders of the young man with the spectacles—'try it out in various places until it wound up in here. Larry's awfully fussy about little things like that, aren't you, Larry? Queer picture, isn't it? One of these days I'm going to get someone down here to explain it to me and tell me if it's worth anything.'

I turned back to face him. He took his arm from Larry's shoulders and put it round Astrid's. He pulled her close to him. Once more he was beaming and boyish.

This seemed a good moment to ask him something that had been on my mind ever since he called me in Houston.

'Mr. Sarrazin,' I said. 'I'm naturally eager to learn why you've asked me to come here. Tell me, exactly what kind of a building is it you want me to design for you?'

'Building?' He grinned. 'What sort of building?' He and Larry looked at each other, as if what I'd said had amused them. 'Oh, I don't want you to design me a building!'

'No?'

'No!'

I frowned. 'Well, what *do* you want me to design, then?'

The brown eyes became slightly opaque without losing anything of their charm or good-nature.

'If I asked you to guess, do you think you'd be able to?'

'Guess?'

'If you tried from here to next week?'

'Mr. Sarrazin . . .'

'Oh please, won't you call me Gabriel?'

I was impatient and couldn't conceal it. He laughed again. He was enjoying himself. I saw that the depths of his eyes were growing quite thick and muddy.

'It's something that'll intrigue you,' he declared. 'I can promise you that!'

'Well?'

'As I said when I called you, you'll find it a challenge . . .'

'What sort of challenge?'

'Why don't you wait and see? We've got the whole of the week-end ahead of us to talk about it.'

I made a sound of such unmistakable irritation that he decided to put me out of my misery, at least partially. He was walking past me, taking Astrid with him. He spoke as they went through the door with a note of amusement and something like triumph in his voice. The Texas accent was slightly more noticeable.

He said:

'It's a maze.'

I stared. 'A . . . a . . . ?'

'That's right.' Another laugh. 'Didn't I say you'd never guess, not if you took all week?'

I thought in my ignorance that he was just playing one of his jokes on me.

He gave a final little bubble of laughter at the look on my face. Then he gave Astrid a peck on the cheek and a proprietorial pat on the bottom and steered her through the door before I could think of anything else.

The bespectacled young man stood back, waiting for

me to pass. His eyes behind their black frames were expressionless.

It seemed a wild and even crazy idea until you became more familiar with El Pardo.

The house wasn't at all what it seemed at first sight. It really did conform to Gabriel's conception of a 'fun place'. I should have remembered the belvedere and the plastic sharks. A maze was exactly what El Pardo needed to round it off. Let me explain.

The drawing-room and the dining-room were neutral and conventional. They were meant to be for orthodox occasions and for orthodox people. For people he thought had stronger stomachs, Gabriel unveiled the extravagant side of his nature. He took me on a conducted tour that same evening, and we continued it the next day and the day after that.

Build a maze! ... The suggestion first began to make sense when I set eyes on the penny-arcade. It was a barn-like room built on behind the house and crammed with extraordinary machines. Some were modern, others were fifty or sixty years old. Gabriel, I discovered, spent hours in this room. He'd start up one or other of the piano-players, mechanical-organs, or juke-boxes that lined the walls. Sometimes he'd start them all up at the same time.

Then he'd plunge his hand into one of the sacks of pennies that were propped against the walls of the arcade and rush about popping them into one slot after another.

The arcade had a glass dome that splashed the whole painted glittering metallic scene with brilliant splotches of crimson, mauve, emerald and orange. Gabriel revelled in it. To the wheezing and puffing of *On the Banks of the Wabash, Paper Doll*, or *Meet Me in St. Louis*, he'd scamper up and down pulling levers and pumping handles. There must have been a couple of dozen fortune-telling machines and tell-your-weight machines. Then there was a series of machines that played out little dramas as soon as you dropped your coin in. One of them was an antique English contraption in which a pair of black gates creaked open to reveal a prison yard with a scaffold in the middle. Little figures representing the prison governor and chaplain jerked their arms and gesticulated, a top-hatted executioner threw a shining silver lever, and the condemned man shot down through the trap and the rope twitched backwards and forwards above the dark aperture. Another English machine of Victorian vintage showed the execution of Mary Queen of Scots. A black velvet curtain parted, the headsman slowly hefted his axe, the blade fell, the royal head plopped into the basket. The wire in the neck by which the head was fastened had been painted bright red to suggest when it dropped that an arc of blood spouted out. Gabriel seemed to be fond of such scenes. Another glass case depicted the beheading of Charles the First outside the Banqueting Hall in Whitehall, a building I'd always admired. Another showed the execution of Louis XVI outside the Louvre. There were deaths in the electric-chair and the gas-chamber. The last pair struck me as distinctly creepy, as I got the definite impression they weren't penny-arcade machines at all, but were specially manufactured. They were smooth and well-oiled in their movements, and when the current went through the victim, or he sniffed the cyanide, the shudders that went through his body were horribly lifelike. Gabriel enjoyed pressing the buttons and watching the miniature tragedies taking place to the accompaniment of *Sweet Adeline* or *Casey Would Dance with the Strawberry Blonde*.

He also made me play for a whole afternoon on the group of machines that featured games played by opposing sides. Little figures clicked ice-hockey sticks backwards and forwards or lashed up and down with stiff right legs in English-style soccer. The object was to propel a ball-bearing into the goal. There was also a baseball game where the batter got three strikes and out. We thumped at the brass handles and Gabriel was elated when he won, and childishly upset when he lost. Or we cranked madly at little wheels that sent race-horses and racing-cars circling a track, urging on our mounts and machines with cries and curses. At first I thought the entire business was pretty silly and only joined in to indulge Gabriel. Then somehow I got fired up and entered into the fun of the thing. Gabriel had that effect on you. It didn't take him long to get other people going his way. He acted like a small boy who'd found somebody new to play with, and I honestly thought he liked me.

We seemed to spend a great deal of our time on the shooting-machines. They had the butts of pistols or the stocks of rifles sticking out of them and you swivelled them to shoot rows of ducks or cats sitting on rooftops. We spent hours popping away. He also had a full-size real-life shooting-gallery in the basement, where I watched him shoot both hand-guns and rifles. He had rows of shotguns and hunting-rifles in glass cases in his gun-room. He loved to display them, handle them, fondle them, lubricate them, work the actions. I didn't take much notice of it at the time. It struck me as just another example of a well-known Texan hang-up.

Apart from these pastimes he had another gallery, upstairs, where the entertainment was more sophisticated. This gallery was kept in total darkness. He loved to take you right over the threshold before he snapped the lights on. What burst on you then was a kind of Aladdin's Cave. The place did in fact resemble a cave because it was provided with walls and dummy buttresses leaning at all angles and painted in different primary colours. It was like walking into the set of a German Expressionist movie — *Caligari*, *Homunculus*, or *The House Without Doors Or Windows*. The ceiling had been lowered to a height of less than eight feet. As in all pastimes associated with Gabriel, there was plenty of noise. He told me later that as a professional plane and instrument maker he was particularly interested in noise. He'd written a thesis at Rice (he was a Ph.D.) on the effect of noise on human physiology. The noise in the gallery was an eerie and resonant blend of electronic computer music.

In niches against the left-hand wall were ranged a score of perpetual-motion machines. It was a collection that any scientific museum would have given its eye-teeth for, since it contained what looked like some very early and valuable specimens. Two that I especially remember were one that had a little fluted glass rod that kept twirling round and round in imitation of a jet of water, and another in which a steel ball ran endlessly up and down a series of brass plates tilting delicately backwards and forwards in response to its weight.

Against the right-hand wall was a row of kinetic sculptures. Like the machines, each had an individual light focused on it, operated by means of an invisible rheostat. The sculpture you were looking at brightened while the ones on each side of it dimmed. Gabriel explained that Donna Vorbeck had a standing order to provide him with unusual examples. He wasn't interested in them as works of art. What interested him was the fact that they resembled complicated and ingenious toys. They were constructed of steel, plastic or plexiglass, and presented images that constantly shifted. Some were arrangements of light, others presented varied effects of refraction or altering perspectives. One of them had geometrical shapes that dropped into different positions as the whole thing revolved on the wall behind it. They were beautiful and precise. It was easy to understand why a man with a technical background would be fascinated by them.

At the far end of the gallery was a row of large black boxes that turned out to be peep-shows. You looked through a pinhole and saw a whole room magically displayed before you. The oldest of them looked like a Dutch interior, another like the parlour of an old-fashioned doll's house, and a third resembled a modishly furnished drawing-room. I stared at this last one a long time while the weird music plunked and mooed away. I stared at it because — inadvertently, of course — the maker had given the room an extraordinary resemblance to the drawing-room of my house in New York. Two tiny puppets representing a man and a woman had been inserted into the room, but for some reason they had fallen over and were lying face down on the rug. The rug was a burgundy colour, oddly like the colour of the rug in my house in Whittier Drive.

Gabriel didn't give me much time to study the peep-shows. He was eager to hustle me out of the gallery and up to the third floor. The third floor was his own personal hideaway. He had a room there that housed his own computer, a product of one of his companies, and when he demonstrated it he proved to me that he had an impressive grasp of mathematics and what looked like a highly individual approach to the possibilities of programming. Most of the top floor, however, was devoted to the lay-out of a model railway. It was the model railway to end all model railways. It ran down corridors and in and out of rooms and contained every item known to the model railway maniac. A few of the locomotives and freight-cars were old and battered, as if they were survivors from Gabriel's childhood. But the model railway was only part of it. In one room was a banked track, a replica of Monza or Indianapolis, round which racing-cars and sports-cars whirled in an amazingly life-like way. And there were colossal armies of model soldiers of every period and nationality. The floor of one room was entirely given over to a tableau depicting the jungles of South-east Asia. American troops were attacking guerrillas. Planes dropped down from the height of the ceiling to deliver imitation napalm, and Gabriel activated a platoon of flame-throwers for my benefit, literally burning up a native village. The battle was enhanced with sound effects played at a deafening pitch over a battery of speakers. And while the village was blazing he photographed it with a polaroid camera, showing me the results with great satisfaction. It all looked real—columns of flame and smoke and burning thatch. There were heaps of photographic equipment lying around. He used it to take photographs of carefully staged racing-car and railroad crashes. Blown-up versions of the more striking photographs were thumbtacked to the surrounding walls. One showed a train with a long string of boxcars leaving a viaduct and dropping into a ravine. It looked frighteningly like an actual disaster.

GABRIEL'S pleasure in his possessions was so child-like and whole-hearted it was easy to overlook its destructive side. That first evening—before he'd shown me his treasures—he made such an effort to charm me that I'd have felt a swine not to try and respond to it.

He didn't drink at dinner, but he'd made a study of wine and vintages and pressed on me a really superb hock followed by a splendid burgundy. He produced a little printed card from his billfold and studied it attentively before making his selections. Later there was a thirty-year-old calvados and a Cuban cigar—an Upmann no less—to round off an excellent meal. I felt very relaxed.

We were waited on by the three young men in blazers. They moved around the dining-room, their hands and faces appearing for a moment in the warm pool of light from the candelabras before melting back into the obscurity beyond. Larry, the senior of the trio, served Gabriel himself, putting down the plates in front of him in a deferential but faintly possessive way. All the time taped music played softly—Boccherini, Telemann, Vivaldi. I don't think Gabriel was any more fond of music than he was of art (though I may—again—have been underrating him) but he had a great sense of how he ought to behave and what was expected of a gentle-man and a millionaire.

Naturally, I was aching to ask questions about the project he'd mentioned. But in a playful way he kept heading me off, so I decided not to press him. In his capricious way he ignored my hints and overtures and steered the conversation in other directions. Astrid sat motionless while he talked, and stared down at her plate. She ate almost nothing.

Chiefly he talked about his parents. He was in a reminiscent mood. Their life-sized portraits hung on either side of the fireplace, separated by the artificial flames that leaped up from a pile of synthetic logs. The portraits were kept apart by the blackened muzzles of a crossed pair of old-fashioned muskets. Their subjects were dressed in the evening clothes of the 1920s, though Gabriel's father, obviously ill-at-ease in his boiled shirt-front and wing collar, managed to suggest the stance and attitude of an earlier age. There was something of the frontiersman about him. He didn't look the sort of man you'd want to pick a quarrel with. His wife was different. She looked almost thirty years younger than he was and a million light years more agreeable and sophisticated. I felt I could have talked to her but not to him. She wore a simple and elegant gown of black velvet with a long train. It was cut low to reveal a generous white-powdered bosom. Her arms were firm and fine. Except for a pair of heavy jet bracelets, she wore no jewellery. The painter was no John Singer Sargent, but he managed to convey an air of poise and assurance. Her hair, drawn back tightly from her forehead and held by silver combs in a great knot on her creamy shoulders, was so black and glossy, and her face so distinctively oval, that it struck me she almost certainly had ancestors who came from south of the Pedernales and the Nueces. Texas, after all, has only been independent for not much more than a century. Her ample body was redolent of pride and sensuality.

A feature of her portrait was that she had insisted on having her only child painted with her. Little Gabriel, in a sailor suit, with short white socks and black leather pumps, stood beside his mother and stared down at us as we sat round the dining-table with big solemn eyes. He leaned against his mother's velvet dress, locked close against the full curve of her hip. The little fellow was literally crushed against her, though he didn't seem to find the awkward stance unpleasant. He looked pleased to be huddled close to her. Her chin was lifted in an attitude of hauteur, almost of maternal defiance, in the direction of her husband's portrait, as if she wished to shield the boy from his father.

I doubt if Joel Sarrazin had ever been cruel to his son. There was humour and a kind of rough tenderness in the mouth beneath the heavy black moustache. Still, from what Gabriel was saying, it might have been a good thing to have been shielded from him in certain of his moods. Gabriel related how his father had killed at least four men in his time. He was extremely entertaining on the subject of the celebrated Kohls County feud of 1898, in which his father took part as a principal while still a very young man. It was then that he had disposed of three of his four victims. The affair masqueraded as the usual quarrel over grazing rights, but it was easy to read between the lines of Gabriel's narrative and divine that it was really a case of *pundonor*, even of simple revenge. I thoroughly enjoyed Gabriel's account of it, which had obviously been polished to a fine point by repeated re-telling. I leaned back in my chair and savoured my calvados. I was amused by this picturesque tale of bloodshed and violence, characteristic of an age that was long dead and buried. He told how his father had shot down the two Levitt brothers by hiding in the bushes outside their house and bushwhacking them, and how he rode down their cousin Bob Everest on the open range. It was stirring stuff. As he spoke he kept his eyes fastened for long periods on the pictures beside the fireplace. I noticed that although he was talking about his father, it was his mother's picture he mostly dwelt on. There was a soft smile on his face, and I supposed that he was amused by the spectacle of himself in his sailor's get-up.

As the story continued, I let my glance stray between the portrait of Isabel Sarrazin and the daughter-in-law who she had never known. I wondered how Isabel would have got on with Astrid. Gabriel told me with engaging directness, during the course of his family reminiscences, that she died in giving birth to a daughter when she was only twenty-nine. The girl was stillborn. He was as frank in mentioning these obstetrical matters as he was in talking about the sex-life of the bull Leonidas. He even told me—with what seemed the same apparent cheerfulness—that his father had been twice married before he'd married his mother and married twice more after her death. He'd loathed both his step-mothers. He seemed more amused than bitter, and embroidered his account with tales of the tricks he'd played on them to make their lives miserable. He was such a bad boy his father had sent him away to military school in Louisiana. He'd hated that too, run away three times, and finally forced them to expel him by setting fire to the dormitories.

After dinner, when we were drinking coffee in the drawing-room and it was already past eleven o'clock, he finally came to the point.

'Well?' he enquired. 'I expect you're about ready by now to talk about this business of the maze?'

I remarked a little testily that I'd been ready to talk about it for the past four hours.

He motioned to Black Spectacles to bring me another Upmann and waited while I lit it. He rose and turned to Astrid.

'Would you like to accompany us, dear?'

'Accompany you?'

'Downstairs.'

She stared at him for a moment, then lifted her hand vaguely towards her forehead.

'Do you mind if I don't? I've got rather a headache. I think I'll go to bed . . . '

He was solicitous. He suggested hot milk and aspirins. He said that he thought she looked a bit washed out when she came in from seeing the foreman's wife that afternoon.

She was faintly impatient.

64

'I'll be all right.' She rose, hesitated, then added: 'I expect I'll be asleep by the time you're ready to come to bed ... '

He nodded. 'I expect so, but I'll just put my head round the door. Just to satisfy myself you're tucked up and asleep ... '

She came across to give my hand a brief formal squeeze. Her hand in mine, I commiserated politely about the headache. I mentioned I'd been rather out of sorts and sleepless myself lately, and offered her one of my sleeping-pills. I told her they were a special prescription. She declined.

'No thanks. It's nothing serious.' She withdrew her hand. 'I hope your room is quite comfortable? Are you sure you have everything you want?'

'Yes, thank you, Mrs. Sarrazin. I hope you'll feel better in the morning ... '

She went out quickly, without looking around.

Gabriel turned to me and sighed. 'I knew she wasn't well. She's been rather overdoing things lately. Did you notice how silent she was at dinner?'

He indicated the other door.

'Shall we be on our way?'

I felt a faint pricking on the back of my neck as I walked down the long drawing-room. Gabriel was ahead of me and Black Spectacles behind me. I dismissed the feeling as childish. There'd been absolutely nothing in Gabriel's behaviour to indicate that he had any idea at all of my relationship with Astrid.

We marched in line astern down a dozen well-lighted corridors. I lost my sense of direction. Then we stopped in front of an elevator. Gabriel pressed the button. The door slid open and we entered.

The elevator started to move downward. The journey only lasted a few seconds. The door slid back and we emerged directly into an underground room about twenty feet square. It was warm, well-carpeted, and softly lit.

It was a vault. A bank vault—not the kind you keep coffins in. There were a couple of antique chairs and a rosewood table, and the atmosphere was cosy. There was piped music down here too, no doubt in accordance with Gabriel's acoustical theories. Or perhaps he simply had an aversion to silence? There were no iron bars or grilles. The place didn't need them. In the wall in front of us was a massive steel door with the glass-covered mechanism of an elaborate time-lock bolted in the centre, like a robot with its intestines protruding. It looked solid and impenetrable.

Gabriel took up a position on one side of the steel door. His smile was genial and eager.

'I won't go into the whole thing deeply until to-morrow,' he said, 'when you're rested and refreshed. Tonight you're tired after your drive. But I thought I'd just give you something to sleep on. Actually, I'm terribly interested in the way the human brain works. Computers, and all that. It's a professional interest as well as a personal one. I'm fascinated by the way the brain functions when it's asleep, the way it can feed problems down into the unconscious and come up next morning with the most extraordinary ideas and solutions. So I thought we might at least get you started on the project on your first night here.' He smiled. 'Who knows

what brilliant notions you'll throw off tomorrow morning at the breakfast table?...'

He tapped at the steel door with his knuckles. It was
so thick it gave off practically no sound.

'Not that there's much to show you inside this thing.
I don't use it. It came with the house. Our original
family place is eighty miles away, at Corinth. El Pardo
was always a thorn in our side. It wasn't a big estate in
itself, but it cut our land practically in half. It was just
big enough to bite into Sarrazin land and stop us becoming a consolidated block. See what I mean?'

I nodded. He leaned back against the rosewood table.
He was taking it very much for granted that I'd already
begun to go along with his plans.

'The family who owned El Pardo wouldn't sell. They
were distant relatives of ours, actually. Second cousins
or something. They'd come here from South Carolina
and persisted in holding on. They weren't poor—not to
start with—and wouldn't be pushed out.' Another smile.
'Used to make my old dad hopping mad. Of course, he
never showed it. He could be patient. Very, very patient.'
The smile widened. 'He got them in the end. In the end
he always got everybody. It took him years to do it but
bit by bit he wore them down. He'd got into oil and
they'd stayed in cattle. Foolish of them. So they handed
him the advantage. The way he went about it was very
ingenious. Finally they had to knuckle under and sell.
Dad got the house and land for a song.' He paused, then
added: 'Of course, the joke was... know who the
original owners were?'

'Who?'

He laughed. 'Why, Astrid's people!'

I stared at him and he laughed again, more loudly.

'Mean to say she never told you?'

'Tell me? Why should she tell me?'

'Oh yes. Sorry! I was forgetting. You've hardly met, have you?'

He pushed himself away from the table.

'This is what I've got in mind. This vault's been empty ever since the Hamiltons left El Pardo. It was empty before they left, as far as that goes — no money to put in it. I own a bank in Houston, so what do I want with a private vault? For years I've been racking my brain for some way to use the thing — it seemed a pity to rip it out. And finally it came to me. I'd been wondering how to round off the entertainments El Pardo's got to offer — the slot-machines, the sculptures, the time-machines and all the rest of it. And somehow the subject of a maze cropped up —'

Here I cut in. I said I didn't see how an out-of-the-way subject like a maze could just 'crop up'.

He smiled. 'I was showing a party round my new computer research plant at Corpus Christi. One of them was a biologist, a very sharp fellow. Over lunch he started comparing a computer with the human brain. That got me interested. He began to describe a series of experiments he was doing at the University of New Mexico. Experiments with rats. In mazes. He'd been struck by the resemblance between the pattern of his mazes and the pattern of the human cortex, with its tangled masses of axons and dendrons, its nerve pathways, its millions of synapses. Rather like a computer, when you come to think of it. Rats in mazes. Fascinating, eh?'

He was talking with the same enthusiasm as that with which he'd talked earlier about his Charollais, or the Kohls County feud. He'd started pacing around the underground room, warming to his subject. I remember the soft lights, the deep beige carpet, the music playing *Someone to Watch Over Me*, the crystalline reflection from the square glass cover of the time-lock, the glint from Larry's spectacles as he waited patiently beside the door of the elevator.

I was only half listening to his voice. I was chewing over the curious fact that Astrid and Gabriel were cousins . . .

' . . . Lots of fun for guests . . . ' I heard him saying. ' . . . Something really unusual . . . Kind of a grand finale . . . It'd be absolutely original – unique. El Pardo'd be celebrated. A great American show place. Imagine it! A genuine, all-out, slap-up, full-blown, full-fledged, whole-hog modern maze. The Eighth Wonder of the Modern World. And who'd have designed it? You would! You'd be the only living architect ever to design and build a structure like that. Doesn't that appeal to you? Isn't that tempting? Isn't that the challenge I promised you?'

He slapped his hand on the glittering steel door of the vault.

'Ideal site . . . guests have dined . . . shoo 'em into the elevator . . . bring 'em down . . . open the door . . . and right there facing them . . . that's when the fun really begins . . . '

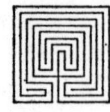

... there facing them ... *dark dark dark dark* ... there facing ... *dark dark* ...

All to pieces now can't pick up lie still wish Leonidas white bull burgundy wish bees lava volcano nightingale wish Lorraine call from phone lie still lie still hold hold on hold hold hold hold on still lie still still hold on hold on ... I will lie still. I will wait patiently till I waken. I will not exhaust myself fighting this nightmare. I will not allow the darkness to drive me mad but I will use the darkness as a screen on which to project my plans.

Now.

I can remember. I will not let the blackness and dryness in my throat and pain in my mouth and pain in my chest and endless insidious noise distract me.

I can remember.

I can remember agreeing to build the maze. I can remember I built it partly because I wanted to and partly against my will. Against Astrid's will. I didn't like the atmosphere of El Pardo and wanted to get away. I wanted to take her away too. I wanted us to make the final break and start on our life together. I kept asking and asking her. We met in secret again and again. I begged and begged her.

What could I do? I accepted the commission to design Gabriel's architectural folly largely because it gave me an excuse to stay at El Pardo and be close to Astrid. I could keep the pressure on her.

But I've got to admit I got down to the job with a genuine relish. Not only was Gabriel a persuasive advocate but I discovered he was right. No architect had been called on to provide this particular commodity for almost two centuries. I took a bright girl called Jenny Anderton out of my office in New York and made her a full-time researcher. I got her to turn up all the material she could on the subject of mazes and labyrinths.

There wasn't much. But what there was was fascinating. The whole history of the maze is extremely ancient. It seems to have derived from the dark and frightening depths of the caves in which our ancestors lived in the Old Stone Age. The interior of these caves could only be reached by narrow winding paths, and it was in these deep and inaccessible places that primitive hunters painted the images of the wild beasts and weird deities they worshipped. The maze might also be a symbol of the great primeval forests in which early man was terrified of losing himself. The old sign of the swastika is a maze pattern. On the wall of the Casa Grande in Arizona is a maze whose centre represents the spiral hole through which the Pima Indians believed they had emerged from the Underworld.

It was in Ancient Egypt that the maze really came into its own. According to Herodotus, the Great Labyrinth of Crocodilopolis was a larger and more impressive structure than the Great Pyramid of Gizeh. He wrote that it had twelve huge covered courts and thirty thousand rooms. Jenny Anderton dug out for me all the references to the Great Labyrinth in classical literature. Strabo, Diodorus Siculus, Pomponius Mela, Pliny, Plutarch— she prepared dope-sheets with extracts from all of them. I remember a striking quotation from Pliny's *Natural History* to the effect that 'some of the passages and rooms are made so that the opening or shutting of a door makes a terrifying sound like thunder, and most of the Great Labyrinth is plunged in perpetual darkness . . . '

The Greeks and Romans took over where the Egyptians left off. Virgil mentions in the *Aeneid* something that he calls 'The Game of Troy' in which horsemen perform intricate operations resembling the windings of a labyrinth. The ceremony spread all over the Mediterranean. It survives in modern dances in Spain and Sardinia and reached even further afield to Scotland and Wales. The Romans were also very fond of incorporating mazes into the designs of their mosaic pavements. A famous example is in the Casa di Labarinto at Pompeii and others are recorded from remains of villas in such places as Tunis, Marseilles, Salzburg, Paris and Caerleon in Wales, the latter associated so closely with the legend of King Arthur. The maze design and the maze dance survived into the Middle Ages in Christian churches. On the floors of more than thirty churches and cathedrals existed pavements laid out in the form of elaborate mazes. These holy mazes could be found at Rome, Ravenna, Cremona, Pavia, Piacenza, Chartres,

Reims, Amiens, Sens, Bayeux, Poitiers. Sir Giles Gilbert Scott restored a maze on the floor of Ely Cathedral in Cambridgeshire as recently as 1870. What purpose did they serve? No one knows. Perhaps they were *Chemins de Jerusalem*. That is, instead of taking the actual road to Jerusalem as a pilgrim or Crusader, it was possible for a devout worshipper to make the journey in his imagination within the precincts of his own church. Perhaps the church mazes were also associated with the idea of penance. If you were a sinner, you would be instructed to go to the *Chemin de Jerusalem* and follow its winding course on your knees. I suppose there was also the idea of following the tricky and tortuous path through the snares of the world until one found oneself finally arriving at the Gates of Paradise.

During the Renaissance and the *ancien régime* mazes maintained their popularity. Entire gardens were laid out in the form of labyrinths. In 1560 Lord Burghley built a maze at his estate at Theobalds, and there was another at Hatfield House. Cardinal Wolsey ordered one to be built at his seat at Hampton Court. The present Hampton Court maze dates from 1690 and was described by Daniel Defoe.

Hampton Court maze was tiny in comparison with the French 'Labyrinthe de Versailles', designed by the great architect Hardouin-Mansart for Louis XIV. This vast maze was furnished with thirty-nine groups of statuary representing incidents in Aesop's *Fables*. The statues were worked by hydraulic machinery activated by fourteen water-wheels driving two hundred and fifty pumps. Sarrazin would have loved the Labyrinthe de

Versailles. It set the Sun King back half a million dollars in modern money. Unfortunately it was completely dismantled in 1775 – but Jenny Anderton found illustrations of it in a book published in Paris in 1677 and written (appropriately) by Charles Perrault, creator of such fairy tales as Cinderella.

I thought the Versailles labyrinth was the model Gabriel would go for. It was ingenious, like his time-machines and kinetic sculptures. It was also expensive, and he wanted the El Pardo labyrinth to be expensive too. It was to be an example of conspicuous consumption. He was prepared to spend three-quarters of a million dollars on his Texas whimsy. But to my surprise the labyrinth he kept referring to again and again was the most renowned one of all. This was the legendary labyrinth of King Minos at Knossos in Crete. Gabriel had evidently been doing some research on his own account. He was well primed about all aspects of the Cretan legend. It occurred to me that it must have been Crete which had set him off on the subject in the first place. He'd probably heard about it from a friend who'd been cruising round the Mediterranean with a Greek millionaire, or from a magazine article.

He'd accumulated a mine of information about it. He'd even gone to the length of collecting specimens of the twelve or thirteen Cretan coins that feature the labyrinth on their reverse side. Some of them were extremely rare and must have cost him a fortune. He carried them round in his hip pocket. As he talked he'd produce one and fondle it, smoothing its silver surface with his thumb. He talked constantly of the labyrinth, dwelling on different details of the story. He brought me references about it from Claudian and Catullus. He produced a passage from Apollodorus that stated that it was modelled on the Great Labyrinth of Egypt.

Its history was certainly colourful. King Minos' wife was called Pasiphaë, and she conceived a monstrous passion for a beautiful white bull. She got the great artist and artificer Daedalus to fashion a simulacrum of a cow into which she could creep in order to position herself to have intercourse with the bull. She became pregnant and in course of time bore a gigantic creature which was half-man and half-bull. Minos then called upon Daedalus to fashion a place where the creature, called the Minotaur, could be imprisoned, and Daedalus conceived and executed the idea of the labyrinth. Later, a son of Minos called Androgeos was killed by a gang of brigands when he was travelling through Attica on a visit to the mainland. His father thereupon laid upon Aegeus, the King of Athens, a tribute to be paid every nine years. It consisted of seven youths and seven maidens, who were sent to Crete to be shut up in the labyrinth and sacrificed to the Minotaur. On one voyage the freight of doomed youths and maidens included Theseus, a son of King Aegeus. At Knossos he fell in love with the beautiful Ariadne, a daughter of Minos, and with her help he penetrated to the centre of the labyrinth, slew the Minotaur, and returned safely to the entrance by using the famous device of the thread of wool. When he returned to Athens he forgot to hoist the white sail his father had asked him to raise if his expedition had gone well. When the poor old king saw the black sail he rushed down the cliffs and threw himself into the sea. The sea has been called the Aegean ever since.

A very dramatic and tragic series of events.

...remember remember remember remember ...

Am I beginning to recover? Drink wearing off? Or drugs or whatever it is?

Any minute now I feel I'm going to wake up. Find myself back in my bedroom at El Pardo. See the blur of light from the window. Make out the gleam of light that comes through the vent of the air conditioning.

I feel better. Less sick. Less dazed. Stronger. Harder. Body seems to belong to me. Dream is dying down. Not that awful sense of dislocation. As if my energy and will-power were starting to trickle back.

And it's getting light. Oh yes, it is.

God almighty, it's growing lighter. Only a softening of the darkness. Tingle on the eyelids. Black ice beginning to snap and melt. Darkness dissolving like chocolate in a pan.

Relax. Slacken your limbs and empty your mind and hoard your strength and wait for the moment when the light is ...

IT took a much shorter time to build the thing than you might have thought. It was a job that under other circumstances I'd have liked to have dawdled over. It would have been fun to have fooled around with it. But Texans aren't that sort of client. They're people in a hurry. And Gabriel for some reason had suddenly become in a greater hurry than most. It seemed he couldn't wait for his new toy to be finished and ready.

We were on very good terms during the nineteen weeks it took me to finish the Great Maze of Texas. We got along very smoothly. He was considerate and courteous and gave me a completely free hand. But for me at least it was bound to be an uneasy association. I was glad that for at least twelve of those nineteen weeks he was dodging around the country in his jet, busy with business affairs — principally a merger between Sarrazin Resources and some mammoth printing company in Indiana.

My first step was to decide what type of structure I wanted to design. I had to choose between a maze that was unicursal (that is, with a single twisting path leading to the centre) or one that was multicursal (offering a number of different paths dividing up at intervals into two or more branches, most of them going in wrong directions and finishing up in dead ends). Most of the early mazes were unicursal — simple affairs intended for childish amusement and not for taxing the brain. This would not have suited Gabriel at all. This type of maze would have provided his guests with a pleasant little saunter to round off their tour of the penny-arcade and the rest of the house. It would have been little more than a stroll along an underground gallery with a number of innocuous features to negotiate on the way.

Gabriel's instructions were quite specific. He pointed out that most of his guests were very shrewd operators who wouldn't mind having their intelligences tickled. It wouldn't even hurt if one or two of them got bogged down, or even well and truly lost for a while. Think of important men like Phil Braxton or Bo Lattimer stuck in a maze, roaring and cussing and fit to be tied! Wouldn't that be rich? Of course, not that they'd have anything to worry about. The place would be provided with a whole regiment of devices to reassure people and keep prodding them forward along the right lines.

So I got out a ground plan and went over it with Gabriel in order to get it formally approved. It was a large multicursal labyrinth of complex and symmetrical design, rather like a gigantic subterranean three-dimensional chessboard. In fact it was a highly elaborated version of one of the Cretan labyrinths depicted on Gabriel's coins. It featured steps or ramps leading up and down from one level to the next, some of them shallow and some of them sudden and steep.

I put Wendell Barratt in personal charge of construction. He wasn't particularly happy about it. Not because of the job itself — that was easy. As a serious-minded and somewhat humourless young man, he simply couldn't understand why I was postponing work on several important projects to devote my energies to something he considered frivolous and downright crazy. He came from Minnesota and had been brought up to disapprove of Texans. But he never questioned my decisions, and contented himself with making a private vow to clear the thing out of the way as speedily as possible.

There weren't many logistical headaches for him to cope with. Gabriel already owned most of the equipment we needed. We only had to employ outside contractors for some of the relatively minor aspects of the job. For example, Gabriel had a fleet of excavators and earthmoving machines at one of his Texas plants. We took down the gates at the entrance to the ranch and widened part of the dirt road through the wood, and the machines duly arrived on their flat-beds from Galveston a day before they were scheduled to go into action. Everything else we asked for reached us with similar promptitude. Wendell was like a dog with two tails. For once a job went off without a single one of the customary foul-ups. I think it shook even his solid nerves a bit.

The maze was to be situated so deeply under the ground that the platoon of excavators went on gouging away day after day, filling the air with their unholy racket. During the first three weeks, the heavy summer rains I'd encountered on my first visit to El Pardo continued. But this was the time when I was largely occupied with finalizing the design, so it didn't greatly inconvenience us. It didn't seem to worry the machines or their operators. The Euclids and Lübeckers and other metal giants went on tearing great gobbets of soil out of the landscape and spewing them on to the dumpers. The whole area to the west side of the house, acres and acres of it, extending from the west wing right to the far-distant fringe of the pinewoods, took on the appearance of a titanic battlefield. Mountains of soil were thrown up over the entire area, as if an army was digging itself in. The dark brown ranges stretched away almost as far as the eye could see. The din was really beyond belief. A huge expanse of lawn, three fruit orchards and the whole of El Pardo's celebrated rose-gardens—a legacy from Gabriel's mother's time—were eliminated, though we intended to replant them when the topsoil was replaced. We meant to bury the maze so far under the earth that no vestige of it would be detectable. There'd be no hint of its existence. Even the vents of the air conditioning and other apparatus would be hidden by groves and bushes. The whereabouts of the great structure would be secret and enigmatic.

I used many of the techniques employed by the specialists who build underground garages. The business of preparing the enormous basement-like construction and pouring the concrete proved to be a colossal undertaking. The scene at El Pardo must have resembled the scene at Hawara when the Egyptian masons were building the Great Labyrinth for the Pharaoh Amenemhat. We also hit a snag which caused us a good deal of amusement. Some of our workmen were always getting lost. Before we capped the maze with its concrete roof it was easy for someone to stand on one or other of the fifty-foot-high towers we erected at intervals round the rim, and give directions to anyone who'd gone astray. If they were very close to the centre it was a bit more difficult. They were lost to the view of the men on the towers. Once or twice workmen got lost for upwards of an hour and all we could hear were their faint yelps as they blundered invisibly round and round. It was like hearing men drowning far out at sea. As a rule they were good humoured about it and put up with the ribbing they got when they emerged. But now and again an elderly workman or an adolescent one would lose his head and panic and be finally brought out in a state of near-collapse. To counter this we rigged up a thick red cord as a guideline down the central corridors leading to the exit. A series of blue cords designated the corridors that fed into the central corridors, and a series of black cords designated dead ends. All a man had to do was follow a blue cord until he came to a red one, then follow that. The system worked very well, and from then on only the dimmest and dopiest workmen got lost.

Gabriel's crews were exceptionally well trained and well disciplined, as was to be expected of employees of Sarrazin Resources. Wendell was a capable organizer and as for me—well—I can flatter myself that I'm pretty calm and clear-headed. I devoted a great deal of thought to the material I was going to use to face the raw concrete walls of the network of passage-ways. Everything was suggested: wood panels, specially treated to withstand the underground damp or warping from the air-conditioning; marble, to be imported from quarries outside Tucson; a newly-developed light porous brick; and sheets of steel. After carrying out a series of tests I chose the latter. I'd reckoned that Gabriel might insist on marble, in view of the close associations of the El Pardo labyrinth with Knossos. But he said he welcomed the modern character steel would give it. Moreover, there was a steel company in Trenton that supplied high-grade products to Sarrazin Resources. Mohner and Lewis would give him a good price on the sheets we required — we'd need several miles of it — and turn it out to the specification we wanted. So Mohner and Lewis received the contract and six weeks later the first consignments began to trundle down the dirt road across the ranch.

The sheets were beautifully cut and even more beautifully finished. They'd been buffed and re-buffed until their surfaces were as shiny as a mirror. I remember the astonishment and admiration of the crews when they lifted them off the trucks and uncrated them in the sharp summer sunlight, laying them on the raw and roughened ground to one side of the mammoth opening in the earth. They whistled as the glittering squares were removed from their individual wrappings, each team handling them as if the were glass, reverently placing them in ten-foot-high stacks with layers of sacking spread carefully between each sheet.

I stayed on the site with Wendell almost continuously, though once or twice, like Gabriel, I had to go away on business trips. One of our biggest headaches, and one for which we ought to have made more adquate preparation, was the national press and television. When they got wind of it they came swarming round like bees. This was a project as ambitious and as remarkable in its own way as Buckminster Fuller's Astrodome over at Houston. There was bound to be keen public excitement about it. One or two reporters got past the vigilance patrols Gabriel had recruited from his factory police, but in the main security was tight and effective. On the other hand you can't keep out helicopters, and to Gabriel's intense fury some excellent aerial shots of the maze in its unroofed stage appeared in the papers and magazines. The pressmen called it one of the marvels of the twentieth century, though they couldn't resist some lofty remarks about Texan extravagance and megalomania. One Sunday one of the television networks even carried a thirty-minute special feature gleaned from various snippets. I tried to explain to Gabriel that you can't expect to build an underground structure the size of several football fields without attracting maximum attention. As he became increasingly enraged, his orders to his private police force became harsher. Several too-inquisitive reporters got bloody noses and broken cameras. One was severely beaten up.

It was on one of these final hectic days as the job was nearing completion that Astrid and I had the last and most frantic of our meetings. Putting up a building is always a struggle. This one was no exception. Her presence at El Pardo became a terrible added strain. She was so close—yet most of the time a million miles away.

We managed to meet in the house or on the estate

two or three times a week. It was easy to exchange whispered messages when we saw each other every day. We'd snatch a few minutes together in an out-of-the-way room or in the sculpture gallery or the summerhouse. There was a secluded spot in the pinewoods near the lake which became a favourite rendezvous. Whenever it was safe to go to the summerhouse we went there because it was there we could make love. It wasn't comfortable or romantic, and all the time we were aware of the distant noise of the work going on on the maze, but being under the same roof had given us a sharp and gnawing sense of physical need.

It was one of these last trips to the summerhouse that produced the urgency of our final meeting. I'd gone up to my room hot and sweaty at the end of a working day and was looking forward to soaking myself in the gold and marble tub. I'd got my jacket and shirt off when the door opened softly and Astrid slipped into the room. She closed the door quietly and ran across the carpet to where I was standing between the bed and the window. She wasn't wearing shoes. She saw my look of surprise. Up to then we'd always been careful. Coming to my room like this was taking a fearful risk. It was true Gabriel was in Missouri on business but his three young men would be lurking somewhere in the background. I moved to the window, grasped the cord that closed the curtains and quickly drew them shut.

Even while I was standing with the cool body in the yellow linen frock in my arms she was murmuring that she could only stay a minute and would have to leave almost at once.

'Don't worry.' I pressed my face into her sweet-smelling hair. 'It'll be easy to invent an excuse. What's so unusual about you're coming into my room for a second to ask me something? I'm practically a member of the family by now, aren't I?'

'Darling, I had to see you. I've been looking for a chance to talk to you since Gabriel left. I couldn't seem to escape from Larry.'

'Where is he now?'

'Out in the drive. He and the others are helping to unload the furniture Gabriel ordered for the party next week.'

'Good. We've got a few minutes.'

We exchanged a long hard kiss. I drew her over to the bed, gently pushed her down and knelt beside her. She relaxed on the coverlet. It was nearly a week since I'd been able to snatch a few moments with her.

'God . . . I've missed you . . .'

She gave herself up eagerly to an embrace, then stirred and struggled upright.

'No . . . no . . . We must talk . . .'

I let her sit up. Much as I hated it I had to admit this wasn't the time or place for lovemaking. She looked up at me, eyes troubled. Something was the matter.

'What is it?'

It wouldn't come at once. She laced her hands in her lap and bowed her head. The room was shadowed now the curtains were drawn. The noise of pile-drivers and jack-hammers filtered in from outside.

Finally she said:

'Darling . . .'

85

She couldn't go on. I cradled her head against my stomach and stroked her face as you'd stroke a troubled child.

'Please, darling—what is it?'

At last she said:

'Darling . . . '

Another pause.

'Well?'

'I . . . I think I'm pregnant . . . '

My fingers tightened on her face. Then they relaxed.

Neither of us moved. Finally I got off the bed and knelt in front of her and forced her to unlock her hands. I took them in mine.

'Does Gabriel know?'

She didn't look up. She gave a little doll-like shake of the head.

I picked my words carefully.

'He doesn't?'

Now she looked up at me.

'It isn't his.'

I said nothing. She frowned, her eyes searching. Her tongue moistened her dry lips.

'I haven't been—*with* him . . . Anyway, it isn't his, because . . . well . . . it *couldn't* be . . . '

'*Couldn't* be?'

'No.'

'How do you mean?'

'I mean he couldn't . . . *can't* . . . '

'*Can't?*'

'No.'

It began to sink in.

86

She said: 'Never . . . not before . . . or ever . . .'

That was it. The meaning of the years of childlessness. Her sexual exigency. The frenzy and abandonment.

Leonidas . . . glasses of milk . . . little boy in a sailor-suit squeezing against an ample female thigh . . .

At that moment I regretted the delicacy which made us avoid talking about Gabriel during our days in Los Angeles and New York. It was something I ought to have known. I should have guessed. I'd done him a worse injury than I'd dreamed of. To deceive a man was one thing . . . to deceive a man who was . . . *well*! At that moment, straddled there above the bed with my arms round her, I didn't like myself much.

'How long have you known?'

'I'm not sure, even now. I suspected about three weeks ago . . . the end of the month.'

'Have you seen anyone?'

'A doctor?'

'Have you?'

She nodded.

'Oh? You have? And?'

'It's too early to be certain.' She paused and said in a voice so low I could hardly catch it: 'If it's true, you—wouldn't be angry with me?'

'Angry? . . . Delighted!'

'Delighted?'

'Of course! Now you'll have to do what I've been asking you since the spring. You'll have to tell him you're leaving him.'

I felt a shudder go through her. She pressed closer against me. I knew that didn't mean she was reluctant to leave him and come to me. But I knew how unwilling she was to hurt him. So why had she let herself have a child? And at this time? It hadn't occurred to me to ask if she was being careful. I thought being pregnant was the one thing she'd be anxious to avoid. Probably she felt that refusing to go the limit made our relationship small and squalid. All the same, I couldn't help asking myself what sort of a situation I'd unknowingly walked into.

Her lips tightened and trembled.

I went on: 'I know you're unhappy about telling Gabriel. I can handle Gabriel.'

To my dismay, she started to cry.

'Hey!...'

'*Handle Gabriel*!...'

Her voice held a note of scorn and fear. My voice hardened.

'Listen, darling...'

'Have you any idea how many men have thought they could "handle Gabriel"?...'

'Look, I'm not an idiot. I've been thinking about things—making plans.'

As happened during almost all our meetings during the past four months, reproaches began pouring out of her about my taking the job at El Pardo in the first place.

I said: 'Darling, what's the use of arguing about all that now?'

She rose and faced me.

'We've got to go away. Tonight.'

'Tonight?'

'That's what I came in to tell you.'

'Darling, you know there's nothing in the world I'd like to do better. But I'm right in the middle of finishing the—'

'Tonight! Before he gets back.'

'Darling, listen to me. There's only another week or so to go. You said yourself the doctor wasn't sure. Why don't we wait at least until after we've had the party?'

'This is the best chance we'll have.'

'Look, we can't hide from him, wherever we go. And what difference do another few days make?'

'You sound as if you want to stay? As if you want to attend that silly party?'

'Well, it's to celebrate the end of the job. And it's not just me—it's for my own men and for Gabriel's men. Everyone who's slogged his guts out on it.'

She was growing increasingly angry and impatient. I tried to calm her down. We stood there arguing, though instinctively keeping our voices down.

'Listen, darling. The day the party's over—the day after!—we'll tell him together and go away. I promise!'

She accused me of vanity. Perhaps it was. I only knew in a dim sort of way that I was genuinely looking forward to the party. It would round off the whole business. There'd be all my own people and seventy or eighty important guests. I'd already seen a list of the invitations. There'd be representatives from television and the other media. It would be a pretty big occasion. It all goes to show how deeply Gabriel had succeeded in hooking me on the idea of the El Pardo Maze.

Oh yes, I was looking forward to that party. Really looking forward to it.

. . . light?

Isn't it getting lighter?

Yes.

I'm coming out of it. Must be the dawn streaming between the curtains of my room.

Party — ?

Last night!

That's it!

Remember when I was dressing in the —

Wait.

Light becoming firmer. Congealing. Objects emerging.

There's someone else. I can see him. Over there!

Another man. The other *man.*

The man who's been following me about — crawling behind me.

Shout!

HEY! You there —'

He's moving. Crawling towards me. On all fours. Like a dog. Big dazed draggled dog. Is he vicious? Coming close . . .!

HEY! . . .

Good God — laughing now. *Hear him laughing.*

Myself *laughing.*

ME. *Just enough to see that it's* ME. *Reflection. Sheets of polished steel. Mohner and Lewis. Buffed like a mirror.*

Hair over sweaty forehead. Eyes burning fever. Shirt. Trousers. No socks. No shoes.

Last phase of the dream. Final fling of the bad trip.

Yes. The light's getting brighter. Only a few seconds more. Bloody thing's dying. So here I am. Silk shirt and evening pants. Scared half to death catching sight of myself in a steel wall.

Can make out the whole corridor now. Very long and very wide. And very high. Beige carpeting. Lights in slits high up in the wall. Convex lenses of the all-seeing eyes. Square glass indicators of the emergency guiding system.

Which way am I going? Towards the entrance? Towards the centre?

Corner. Don't know what good I'm doing just aimlessly walk . . .

ASTRID!

WHEN I saw her sitting on the floor, her back propped against the steel wall, I knew I wasn't going to wake up. I wasn't going to wake up because I hadn't been asleep. Everything clicked into focus. There hadn't been any sleeping tablets. There hadn't been too many martinis. There hadn't been any nightmare. It wasn't any bad dream I'd been having. The dream wasn't a dream at all. The dream was real.

I'd been down there all the time. *In the maze*. Gabriel had done the crazy thing I'd always had a vague idea — but *only* a vague idea — he might do.

She was slumped down in an attitude of despair. She looked sick and defeated. She didn't hear me approach because of the thickness of the carpet (oh no, her husband hadn't spared any expense!). She didn't see me because her head was turned away, lolling on her shoulder as if her neck had snapped. Her fair hair, which had been elaborately arranged, broke and fell in an untidy wave across her face. She wore only a silver-coloured negligée and her legs and feet were bare. On her finger was the sapphire ring from Arpels and Van Cleef.

I knelt down in front of her. Her eyes were closed. I could smell a sharp perfume on her skin. Her lipstick and mascara had been carefully applied but the sweat on her face had smudged them. I was afraid of frightening her. When I put out a hand and touched her naked shoulder I did so as lightly as I could. No response. My own heart was beating fast and I was in a state of semi-shock. I still hadn't recovered from the terror of waking to a state of things more fantastic than any I could have experienced in a dream. I cupped my hands beneath her chin and pulled her head sharply towards me.

Her eyelids fluttered and opened. She gave a little weak gasp.

I leaned forward. She shrank away, as if the rapidly brightening light was hurting her eyes.

My voice was like a stranger's. It was harsh and remote and I could hardly believe that it was mine.

'It was you? In the darkness? It was you I could hear? . . . '

I had to wait for what seemed hours before she answered.

'I guessed it was you . . . ' Her voice was as different-sounding as mine. 'I tried to keep up . . . You were going so fast . . . '

My head was throbbing. I squeezed my eyes shut and kneaded the nape of my neck. I had to throw off this dizziness. I had to start thinking clearly.

She sat upright. Suddenly there was a harder if still trembling note in her voice.

'I told you! Didn't I tell you? Would you listen to me? Didn't I beg you to be careful?'

I lowered myself to the carpet, watching her. She was still drowsy but a little more awake now. Like me, she was starting to snap out of what she must have taken for her own bad dream. I tried to sound reasonable but my voice was still shaking.

'Darling, I *was* careful. I never said a word or gave a hint . . . '

'I tried to warn you! I did! Didn't you realize the risks we were running?'

I reached forward and caught her arms. They were sweaty and clammy. I gripped them fiercely.

'We'll get out of this.'

'How? You imagine he hasn't thought of everything? Every twist and turn? You don't know him!'

'We'll get OUT of this!'

'Remember what you said?—about "handling Gabriel"? Well—Gabriel's handling YOU!'

'Oh no, he isn't! I'm not stupid—I guessed a long time ago he might let his lunatic sense of humour run away with him. So I've taken care of that.'

'Oh? How?'

'Never mind! Whatever he's up to, does he really think he can ever get away with anything as mad as . . . '

'He *is* mad! Don't you see? He *is* mad! Do you think I've lived with him all this time and I don't know? Do you think I didn't know it when I was a girl and his vicious old father swindled us and drove us out of El Pardo? Didn't you see I was doing everything I could to . . . '

I shook her.

'Listen! If he thinks he's going to scare us . . . '

'You think he only means to *scare* us?'

'*Listen*, will you? This is just another of his silly stunts, that's all. Another of his silly tricks.'

'If you think it's just a . . . '

'Do you honestly think he'd risk everything? Sarrazin Resources? Throw everything away?'

'He'll have *considered* all that.'

Her words brought back to me the memory of the computer on the top floor. I remembered the bright metal chessmen in the drawing-room.

When she started to talk hysterically I shook her again to silence her.

'All right! Perhaps he *is* mad. But I promise when we get out of here . . .'

'Get out of here? We aren't going to get out of here.'

'I wish you'd *listen* to me . . .'

'You know what he's done? He's made you build a trap for yourself! Build a tomb for yourself! For both of us.'

She started to laugh. I felt my face go cold.

Rats . . . in mazes . . .

I scrambled to my feet and looked down at her. I was frightened but angry too.

'We're wasting time and energy. The sooner we give this thing some thought the sooner we'll be out of here. The sooner I can tell that maniac . . .'

She heaved her body upright against the wall and shouted:

'There's nothing you'll tell him! Nothing! Ever!'

'Oh, come on, darling — this is simply one of his sick jokes!'

I tried to smile. But I knew she was right. Automatically I lifted my eyes and looked at the ceiling. In contrast to the brilliant metal walls the roughcast concrete of the ceiling had been painted a jet black. Set into the centre was the round eye of one of the scanners. The ceiling was five feet thick. It was reinforced, stressed with steel mesh, criss-crossed by internal ducts that carried wires for the heating and lighting and dozens of other things. And on top of the five feet of concrete was eight feet of red Texas earth. I'd had the mountains of soil from the excavations shovelled back into place by the squadron of bulldozers. I'd had them flattened and rolled and tamped down ready to be sown with grass seed and planted with shrubs.

She was following my glance. She'd often visited the site and seen what was going on. The same thoughts were going through her mind too. I cursed myself for accidentally underscoring the full misery of the jam we were in. From now on I'd have to try and stop reminding her of the basic horror of the situation.

A muscle in her neck was quivering like a tiny animal. I reached down and took hold of her hands. Like her arms they were clammy, in spite of the fact that the temperature down here was warm. She got up and followed me down the corridor. She walked almost meekly and dragged one bare foot after the other. All at once she stopped.

'What time is it?'

I didn't answer. I kept urging her along.

'What *time* is it?'

It was a pointless question. What difference did it make what time it was? Anyway, I didn't know. It could be morning, afternoon or midnight. There *was* no time down here. The only time that existed was the time it would take us to die.

I'll confess that at that moment I was tempted to give up the idea of struggling and fighting back. I was still weak. Why inflict on ourselves all that pointless torture? Wouldn't it be less painful to lie down in the corridor and wait for the end? Gabriel held every one of the cards. He'd thought it all through. He'd had the nineteen weeks it took us to build the maze to make his plans foolproof. Probably he'd been working on the idea for months before that. Somehow he must have found out about Astrid and me.

I was bruised in body and mind. I knew now the pain in my mouth and chest were the result of a desultory beating-up I must have received when I was lying unconscious, either down here or upstairs in my bedroom. A few casual contemptuous kicks in the face and ribs. Touching these painful spots, I was suddenly aware of the first stirrings of the desire to hit back. I wouldn't let him get away with it. He'd better make sure I never got out of here, because if I did I was going to make him sorry he'd ever picked up that phone and called me at South Main Street.

Astrid was asking what time it was because she was trying to orientate herself. She was groping towards reality. A healthy sign. The first step was to start thinking rationally. We'd go back to the beginning and try and unravel what happened. It would make us feel we'd got back on a logical track.

I was guiding her down the corridor. I wanted to reach a point where we'd be out of range of the scanners in the ceiling. Also out of range of the sensitive microphones associated with them. The scanners were placed at strategic intervals. Usually there was one to a corridor, but in some of the longer corridors there were two, one at each end. There was usually a slight gap in the middle where the scanners failed to overlap. I was pretty certain someone – Gabriel or Larry – was watching us. If I couldn't stop them watching us, at least I could get us more or less out of earshot.

I whispered to her to keep her voice down. The inane music was still blaring out. Now it was a bright Strauss-type polka. Probably Gabriel made his selections precisely because of their incongruity and irony. Well, it could also serve to drown what we were saying to each other. I squatted down and motioned to her to do the same.

I said quietly: 'Let's try and reconstruct what happened. At least it'll give us a starting-point.' I put my hand on her arm. Again I caught the mingled smell of sweat and perfume. 'Think back. When did it start?' I smoothed the long hair from her cheeks and forehead. 'Come on, darling – help me . . . '

She raised her head. She saw the bruising round my swollen mouth and put out a hand to touch it.

'It's all right. They didn't hit me hard. They wanted to save me for . . . well . . . ' I stroked her hand. 'Think. Where did it start?'

She spoke in a thick whisper. 'The party . . . '

'Yes – the party!'

'He must have had it all worked out . . . '

'That's right – he got me down here by means of a trick . . . I remember now – some of it, at least . . . '

Why did I fall for it? If he'd tried to spring the party

on us unexpectedly—at the last minute—we wouldn't
have been caught so easily. But it was made to look so
authentic. From what we now told each other, I could
piece together the whole picture. To begin with, there
were the invitations to the private pre-opening festivities.
The invitations had been specially printed a month in
advance. They were large, handsome, deckle-edged, on
hand-made paper, inscribed in gold. And like the busy
preparations for the party they were nothing but an
elaborate fake. He must have put everybody off but us
two at the very last moment.

I realized now why I'd been so surprised when I drove
up to the house and saw that no other guests had arrived.
I'd received a sudden summons before breakfast that
day to drive to San Antonio to see a prospective new
client—who was one of Gabriel's closest friends. True, I'd
driven back somewhat early in my anxiety to get ready
and my customary anxiety to see Astrid: but I thought a
few cars at least might already have been parked in the
driveway. And why wasn't a small crowd of commen-
tators and cameramen setting up their equipment and
getting ready to get down to business? The media had
agreed to hold off until the gala opening in return for
special facilities.

Two of Gabriel's young men appeared with their usual
creepy promptitude to park my car. I suppose Astrid
was right about there being an electric eye at the main
gates. One of them carried my briefcase up to my room.
It had all become such routine procedure that I suppose
I'd been lulled into a state of mind where I thought
nothing dramatic was ever likely to happen. I was just

getting out a dress-shirt and putting the studs and links in when Larry walked in with a silver tray. On the tray was a frosted glass and a welcome pitcher of the famous El Pardo martini, to which over the weeks I'd become very partial.

We'd never been exactly pally, but I'd got used to seeing him around. I greeted him in a friendly enough way and made some casual conversation about the big evening that lay ahead. The ice tinkled pleasantly in the pitcher. I actually asked him to pour the drink for me. I asked him when the other guests would be turning up. He made a noncommital reply that must have satisfied me. I remembered lifting the glass to my lips and taking a lingering mouthful.

I took the damned thing into the bathroom and finished it while I shaved and showered. I remember I'd progressed as far as putting my shirt and pants on and was sitting on the edge of the bed fiddling with a sock when it finally got to me . . .

In fierce whispers, huddled there on the carpet, we sorted out the probable course of events. There were a few unavoidable gaps, but it gave us a foundation to build on. It stopped us feeling our troubles had been inflicted on us by some sort of supernatural agency. It reminded us that we weren't victims of divine justice but the victims of Gabriel Sarrazin. Trying to fill in the gaps got us going again, bringing back the feeling of continuity we needed if we were going to try to work out a plan of action.

'How did he manage it in your case, darling?'

I'd come to the end of my story and wanted to hear

hers. She'd grown increasingly attentive as the recital went on, fascinated by her husband's ingenuity and duplicity.

'Did he treat you in the same way?' I asked. 'Did he slip something in your drink? Or did he call the boys and tell them to drag you down here kicking and screaming?'

She pulled herself up, shocked at this idea.

'Oh no! You don't understand! It's hard to explain'— she was pleading with me—'he's always been—well— shy with me ... tender ... even these last few weeks ..'

'Shy?'

'Yes.'

'Tender?'

'Yes! ... even though he ... couldn't ...'

I said abruptly: 'Well, what happened then? Did he just put a little pill in your drink, as he did with me?'

She was frowning, trying to recall. 'I was sitting in front of my mirror ... making up my face ... putting on my earrings ... Larry brought me a drink ...'..

'Ah!'

'I was just about to get dressed and go downstairs ...'

'You'd made all the preparations for the party?'

'Oh no—Gabriel did all that himself.'

'I see!'

'He did it weeks ago.'

I said: 'Darling, listen. I want you to sit here while I go and check on something.'

'Check?'

'I've got to walk a slight distance ... only thirty or

forty yards ... but I'll have to leave this corridor and
go into the next one.'

'You mean — leave me here?'

'Don't worry, we won't get separated.'

'Please, darling — don't go ...'

'Honestly, it won't be for more than a minute.'

She was agitated and tried to get up. I had to force her
to stay where she was. I told her to keep her voice down
and repeated that I wouldn't be long. I didn't blame her
for feeling terrified. The previous week Gabriel had
brought her down here to show it to her. He'd told her
funny stories about the workmen who'd got lost. At one
point he'd pretended he'd lost his own bearings and
couldn't find the way. Considering what he'd already
got in store for her, he must have spent a very amusing
afternoon.

I could have taken her with me easily enough. But I
wanted to try out the emergency devices. If they weren't
functioning I wanted to spare her the added sense of
hopelessness that would result. I hurried down the
corridor and turned the corner. I was confronted with a
fan-like junction of three corridors, all of them stretching
wide, bright, empty, inviting — and treacherous. I stopped
and considered. Easy enough to promise Astrid I wouldn't
get lost. I resolved that I wouldn't go too far. I'd give up
immediately there looked like complications. I took the
left-hand corridor.

To my relief, a few yards down on the right-hand side
I found what I was looking for. On a small red-painted
panel on the wall was a shiny black button. Eighteen
inches above it were two small glass squares. When you

pressed the button a light came on behind one of the squares, either a green light or a red light. On each light was an arrow, one pointing one way, one the other. Anyone who was lost or felt anxious could press the button. The green light showed him he was on the right path and the green arrow showed him which way to go. If the red light came on, the red arrow sent him back the way he'd come, in the direction of the previous button. He kept on pressing buttons until he found the right one.

I pressed the button.

Nothing.

I expected that.

If anyone became completely muddled and started to lose their nerve, they could press one of the alarm buttons. These were red buttons that set off a buzzer in the anteroom upstairs. Someone was always supposed to be on duty up there at the control-panel when the maze was occupied. The controller then acted to guide the person concerned out of the maze as quickly as possible, switching on the microphone-system to do so. Naturally, it was considered a confession of failure to push the alarm. It was regarded as chickening out. Gabriel would treat anyone who begged to be led out of the maze with merciless jocularity. The person concerned would never be allowed to live it down.

I pressed the button.

Nothing.

Dead.

Press.

Nothing.

Dead.

So much for my routine safety-devices. There were also a few private ones I'd installed on my own account. I'd have been a fool if I hadn't had some inkling that Gabriel might try and subject me and some of his other friends or colleagues to one or other of his little pleasantries.

To start with, there were the tiny adhesive tags I'd placed low down on the wall in the main corridor, an inch above the carpet. Second, there were the panels that covered up a number of short-cuts to the exit. These were marked on the control-panel, and people who got lost could be directed to them. They swung open on stiff hinges.

I saw clearly how during my 'nightmare' I'd been groping round for these private devices. The fact that I hadn't found them didn't mean they weren't there. I'd hardly been in a proper condition to look for them. Still, the signs were that Gabriel had been making meticulous preparations. He wouldn't have overlooked any of the minor details.

I was standing there, dejected, staring at the useless red button, when I heard Astrid's voice. She was calling my name in a frantic way that told me she must be running. I swung round in the direction her voice was coming from. I was afraid she might run down the wrong path at the junction and we'd get separated. That was the principal fear that was bound to haunt us.

I barely reached the corner of the corridor when she ran into my arms. I caught her and held her fast. She dug her face into my shoulder and I put my face against her hair, hard and springy with lacquer, trying to calm her down.

'Darling . . . it's all right . . . I was coming back . . . another minute and I'd . . . '

I broke off as I felt her suddenly go rigid in my arms. There was a violent ear-splitting electronic wail from the loudspeakers: a high-pitched nerve-scraping squeal. It was so fiendish-sounding it made us catch our breath.

It lasted ten long seconds, then stopped. Dead silence. For the first time there was no music. Complete absence of sound. The silence was so dense and palpable I'd almost have welcomed the return of the brittle music of the waltz.

We waited.

A voice came over the speaker. At first it was distorted, then the level was adjusted until it came through crystalline and sibilant.

Gabriel spoke slowly.

'Well . . . well . . . well!'

He was making what immediately struck me as a highly unnatural attempt at self-control.

'As you both know, I'm not fond of parties. Still, I'm not a spoilsport, either. I like to see people enjoying themselves. So why should I rob you of the pleasure of your little party? We'll have a little private celebration party of our own, shall we?'

Astrid was beginning to tremble. I folded my arms round her more tightly.

'I don't intend to bore you with any long speeches . . .'

Suddenly he spoke her name. The syllables came out like two cracks of a pistol. She jumped.

'What attracted you to your friend there? His good looks? His cleverness? If he's so clever, let's see how he's going to help you now, shall we?'

The metal walls made his voice whine eerily.

'*You* weren't very clever, were you, my dear?'

She was about to cry out. I pressed my hand over her mouth. I knew this was going to be a war of attrition. We'd last only as long as we could stop him breaking our nerve.

'Shall I tell you how you slipped up? Shall I tell you how many mistakes you made? That little business in Los Angeles—when someone got into your friend's house and stole a television set? Did you really think that was due to a thief or a casual prowler?'

She moved in my arms. I kept my hand in place and gripped her more firmly. I wasn't going to let her plead or argue with him. I knew in my bones there wasn't much point. It had all gone much too far for him to turn us loose.

'And what about your visit to New York? You think it wasn't easy to find out where you were? To hire someone to check on your trips to museums, concerts, restaurants? And how about that sapphire ring you've got on your finger? How did I find out about that? No, I didn't look in your jewel case. You didn't quite reduce me to that. Your cousin Donna told me. Not intentionally. Blurted it out, in her usual chatty way. Told me how generous I was to be always buying you jewels like that. So I checked up on that, too. How many stores do you think there are that sell sapphires of that size?'

Astrid had relaxed as the monologue went on. Cautiously I removed my hand. I then did something that surprised her. I kissed her. I pulled her hard against me, crushed my mouth on hers and held it there while Gabriel went on talking. He spoke more quickly now. The self-control was wearing thin. I'd never heard him like that. I could have sworn that for once he'd spiked up his glass of milk with gin or vodka. Strangely enough, his speech didn't fill me with increased fear but with a sense of elation. He was making his first tactical error.

'Of course, once I'd encouraged Donna to gossip – it doesn't take much doing – other things came out too. Who made that stupid remark about the husband being the last to know? You imagine I didn't discover why you sneaked off three days ago to Dallas to see that Doctor Richtersveld?'

He was beginning to sound overwrought and confused, unable to control the intensity of his emotion. He was directing his monologue only to Astrid. He couldn't bring himself to acknowledge my existence. He was going to wipe me out like one of his tin soldiers.

Then he did an extraordinary thing. He stopped talking and started to play back the tape of a series of conversations. At first, I didn't recognize the voices. A man and a woman were exchanging disjointed remarks with long gaps in between. '... *Don't touch it! ... Set off the WHAT? ... Find it? He MADE it! ... Isn't his because it – well – COULDN'T be ... I mean he COULDN'T – CAN'T ...*' Then I knew what it was. It was a composite tape of the conversations I'd had with

Astrid in the previous weeks. Conversations in the summerhouse, the sculpture gallery, the drawing-room, my bedroom. He'd had the whole damned place wired. He'd known what was going on right from that first afternoon.

I could imagine him seated up there in the control-room. I'd had the steel bars in the vault removed and it was now a pleasant room, most of it taken up by the giant control-panel. I'd kept the massive steel door and the time-lock. They looked mysterious and intriguing. The panel contained the warning-lights and alarm-buzzer, the speaker-system and television screen. It also incorporated a special system in which beads of light moved around a plan of the maze, showing the operator how any or all of the people inside were making progress.

Gabriel would be sitting there, glowering at the screen, preparing to go on mouthing his diatribe into the microphone. On the wall behind I could visualize the mounted heads of a row of stags he'd stalked and shot surrounded by the antlers of a host of smaller horned animals. Beneath was a pedestal with a bronze statue of a Texas longhorn steer. He'd had it brought down from his study to ornament the control-room.

He allowed the tape to run through to the end, even though it must have caused him bitter torment. For some reason he hadn't even cut out passages recording our love-making in the belvedere. But hardly was it finished when his voice came pouring back through the microphone, thick and agitated. Trying to cling to a last pathetic shred of control, he abused and threatened us. There followed a turbid passage about how the Sarrazins clung to their own, how nobody had ever taken away from them anything that was theirs. Then came a garbled rigmarole about divorce. There'd be no divorce. He went on and on about divorce. I realized he was terrified at the prospect of the legal proceedings and the personal revelations that might get dragged out in public. That was why he was now making quite certain that the only two people in the world who knew those intimate private details would never be able to open their mouths. It was curious to hear a definite note of appeal and suffering in the way he talked to Astrid. He was a little boy in a trantrum stamping and dancing on his favourite toy.

Then he started to weep. His voice was shaken by sobs. The microphone enlarged it to a primitive screech. At any other time it would have been embarrassing: now it was frightening. Astrid and I stared at each other at a loss. I put my finger to my lips and motioned her to keep quiet. I reached down for her hand, grasped it, and drew her away in the direction of the corridor we'd been standing in originally. While he'd been talking I'd been trying to use my brains, striving to think of something construc-tive. And I'd noticed something encouraging. Gabriel was shouting about a red thread—about us not having a red thread to help us now. He sounded on the verge of going out of his mind. He seemed on the point of exhaustion: and it was at this stage his voice began to die away, as if he couldn't go on any longer. And as his voice tailed off, so the lights began to dim. It was almost imperceptible, but both of us noticed it.

I hurried her along more rapidly.

She said breathlessly:

'Where are we going?'

I'd happened to notice that the chrome ring round one of the tell-tale eyes in the ceiling above us had been cheap and rough in texture. That told me one thing: that we couldn't be far from the entrance. The light was growing dimmer as I hustled Astrid along and kept my eyes fixed on the ceiling.

Yes! The chrome round the ring on the next light was also rough-textured. I knew there were only five or six rings of that type. All the other thousand-odd in the maze were smooth and shiny. The small number with the rough finish had been included by mistake in one particular batch. We'd put them on the lights nearest the entrance so as to make it easier to replace them when the proper rings arrived.

So it stood to reason that we weren't far from the vault door. What's more, they'd hardly have bothered to drag two drugged people too far into the maze. They'd simply haul us a little way in, then drop us. There was no need to do more.

I also realized why we were only partially clothed. They'd stripped us of anything which might have been of conceivable use to us. My pockets had been emptied. I had no keys, no coins, no penknife. No wristwatch or comb. We had been deprived of anything that with a little ingenuity might remotely have served as a tool or a weapon. I was rather surprised they hadn't pitched us in there stark naked while they were at it—except that I suppose Gabriel wouldn't have been able to bear the sight of it.

But, of course, he also had a practical consideration.

It's not easy to put clothes on a corpse — especially a corpse whose limbs might already be growing rigid. What he intended to do, I guessed, was to let us die. Then he'd enter the maze, find our bodies, and chuck down the rest of our clothing in a heap beside us. Then he'd leave. Next week, next month, even next year, our putrescent bodies would be discovered — by someone else, not by *him*. Perhaps by the first group of innocent visitors to the maze. The police, the public and Gabriel's friends would suppose that, unable to slake our appetites anywhere else in the house, we'd crept down into the maze. After all, it was warm and well carpeted. And the iron door of the vault had somehow slammed shut on us . . . As for Gabriel, he wouldn't know a thing about it. He'd thought Astrid was visiting her sister in California, and that I was away on business. Or if pressed harder, he could say he knew we'd fallen in love and assumed we'd run away together. Sympathy all round. Better to be taken for a husband who's been deceived by a worthless wife and a treacherous Yankee, than a husband who's been deceived because he's impotent. There wouldn't even be any marks on our bodies, except for some superficial bruising round my mouth and ribs, which could be easily explained and might in any case disappear during the first stages of decomposition. I saw now why I hadn't been kicked and beaten more thoroughly . . .

We'd reached the entrance of the maze. It had only taken us a couple of minutes, perhaps less, after I'd spotted those chrome rings.

The door of the vault was shut fast. I went up the five steps and gave it a half-hearted push with my shoulder.

It didn't budge a millimetre. It was thirty inches thick and made of armoured steel. The slab of smooth cold metal, glistening in the slowly fading light, was like the marble door of a mausoleum.

I placed my hands wide apart on the door, gave it another shove, then let my head drop forward with an air of defeat. It was a convincing performance. I wanted Gabriel to see me on the monitor screen and think I was in the process of giving up. It would make him happy. It would also give him a false sense of security. True, it wasn't a difficult part to act: I wasn't exactly brimming over with good cheer. But beneath my drooping exterior I was tingling with suppressed excitement. In another minute or two I'd know whether we'd received a brief reprieve or whether our one and only chance was gone . . .

I bumped my way heavily down the five steps and dropped down on the bottom one, propping my head in my hands. When Astrid sat down beside me and laid a shaking hand one my forearm, I whispered, '*Ssssh! . . . Keep still!*'

I was waiting for the lights to fade away completely. I couldn't move till then. It seemed to take an age for them to dwindle and die out. I fastened my eyes on my bare left foot and kept as still as I could. I was reminded how thirsty I was. Hungry, too. God knows how long it had been since either of us had had anything to eat or drink.

When the last glimmer of light had gone I forced myself to sit still a minute or two longer. Then I slid off the bottom step and lay full length on the ground. I could hear Astrid's light and shallow breath above me

in the darkness and smell the warm spice of flesh and
perfume.

What I was searching for was one of the steel screws
that held the polished metal plate on to the concrete riser.
Everywhere in the maze the drab surface of the basic
concrete was disguised by steel, carpet or paint. I fumbled
frantically for the screw and found its domed outline. It
felt enormous in the darkness. What I was looking for
was behind that metal plate. And here was the snag. I'd
taken care to tighten up the screw only very lightly — but
without a screwdriver I was helpless. I groped for the
second screw, at the other end. Same thing. Impossible
to turn it with a thumb and forefinger.

Now I was really beginning to sweat. Could an over-
conscientious workman have been doing a last-minute
check, found those two slack screws and tightened them?
Our lives depended on my ability to get into the space
behind that panel. I could feel my heart pumping crazily
in my chest. My tongue felt several sizes too large for my
mouth.

I scrabbled at both screws in turn with my nails. Useless. I was glad Astrid couldn't see the look on my face.

She whispered:

'What are you doing?'

I hunched myself on to my knees.

'Astrid.'

'Yes?'

'Your bra.'

'What?'

'Take it off.'

'My . . . ?!'

113

'Take it off and give it me.'

She didn't argue. A bare thigh or forearm—something too firm to be a breast—brushed across my shoulder as she twisted and reached behind her to unfasten the bra. Her hand struck my neck as she handed it to me. It was lacy and warm. We bumped into each other in a soft tangle and it took a second to straighten ourselves out. In the confusion I dropped the bra, feeling a little flare of panic as I brushed my hands over the carpeted floor. A crazy spurt of release flowed through me as my fingers closed over it. On that ridiculous scrap of fabric hung whatever future we had.

My fingertips explored the straps and found what they were looking for. The bra was fastened by means of a small flat metal tag. I let out my breath in a sigh. If it had been fastened by hook-and-eye, we would have been done for.

Grasping the tag, I put out my other hand. I knocked against the metal plate as I searched for the first screw. I guided the corner of the tag into the slot of the screw and gave it a gentle twist. It wasn't easy to manipulate, since it was a Philips screw and the blackness didn't make the operation easier. If the screw had really been tightened by a workman that would have been the end of it. The little tag would have buckled and snapped.

The screw yielded. My spirits gave a jump. No one had tampered with the plate. No one had detected my hiding-place. And it had been right under their noses. They'd made a clean sweep of all the other safety-devices. This one they'd missed. I'd noticed there were hollows under each of the five steps. I did nothing at that time. I'd waited. Only when I had a chance to slip into the maze on my own, late one night, had I unfastened one of the metal plates fixed over the hollow batten behind. By that time I'd fathomed the peculiar nature of Gabriel's mind. I'd realized it was best to prepare for emergencies. Naturally, I'd never dreamed his imagination would carry him as far as homicide.

All the same, I was still desperately anxious as I inserted my hand under the step. What if the bundle wrapped in the duster wasn't there. What if that sadistic bastard or one of his cronies had removed it?

Ah! . . .

My fingers encountered the solid bulk of the cloth. I drew it out and deposited it gently on one of the steps. My fingers were trembling. I made myself replace the panel and screw it back in position. I was so impatient I dropped one of the screws twice. It was important that Gabriel and the others shouldn't learn I was no longer utterly defenceless.

I unwrapped the bundle. My eager fingers explored the contents. Everything was there. Everything. All the objects I'd taken at random from the trunk and glove-compartment of the Maserati and rolled in the duster. I could feel the outlines of the flashlight, the two screw-drivers, the hammer with the long rubber-covered handle. I wished I'd included the whole tool-kit while I'd been about it. I could also feel the cold outline of the slender key. I'd slipped it into the bundle at the last moment, prompted by some obscure but inspired impulse.

Kneeling upright, I placed all these objects in my

trouser-pockets. In the right-hand pocket I put the duster, screwdrivers, and hammer, handle down. In the left I put the flashlight and also the key, pushing the key right down to the bottom where I thought it would be safe. The flashlight had a ring with a length of the tape architects use to tie up their papers threaded through it. I always liked to provide my flashlights with a loop for safety. I wasn't going to use the flashlight till I had to, not only to save the batteries but because its beam would show up on the monitor in the control-room. Gabriel had done us a favour by extinguishing the lights. He could no longer keep track of our position. It gave me an odd feeling to think that he was seated less than a dozen feet away from us — on the other side of a wall as thick as a medieval castle, behind an iron door that wouldn't have been out of place at Fort Knox.

The chief thing now was to put as much distance between us as swiftly as possible. I scraped round on the carpet and picked up the bra. I gave it back to Astrid, inadvertently hitting her on the temple or cheekbone as I did so. There wasn't much point in giving her the bra, or in her putting it on again. Still, perhaps she'd feel a fraction less naked and helpless if she did so. She panted as she wrestled with the thing, an unmistakable taint of fear in the irregular heaving of her breath. But so far she was holding up well. She'd schooled herself to trust me. When she heard the soft clinking of the tools as I took them out of the duster she hadn't uttered a sound, though she must have wondered what was going on.

I got to my feet and reached down and pulled her upright. The worst part of our ordeal now lay ahead of us.

We had to traverse the maze. I felt deeply contrite for having involved her in this mess. I drew her to me and started to run my hands down her body, murmuring endearments and words of encouragement. I held her hard against me and pinned her arms in a rough embrace. In the darkness her body seemed enormous, the body of a giantess, huge and indeterminate. I felt her mouth straining to meet mine. I had a silly feeling Gabriel could see us, almost stretch out and touch us, watch my hand stroking her shoulders, the curve of her buttocks, her thighs, reach round to touch the breasts and belly. Serve him bloody well right. I'd given up the luxury of feeling sorry for him. The body pressed against mine gave me a measure of the strength and reassurance I needed.

I gave her shoulder a last gentle pat. Her body felt less chilled and had stopped trembling. I ran my right hand down her arm and grasped her left wrist. I locked my fingers firmly round it. I felt her arm grow taut but kept my grip in place. She'd have to grow used to it. We'd got several miles to walk in total darkness.

I shuffled a couple of steps away from the door with my free hand in front of me. I was feeling for the wall. When I made contact, I began to walk forward into the maze with my palm brushing the cold surface of the steel. That was my plan. I'd follow the left-hand wall until it brought me to my first objective. It wasn't much of a plan: not very subtle: but it was the only one I had. By using the torch I might have been able to halve the time. Equally I could have got lost. Of course, in previous weeks I'd been used to breezing through the maze. At first I'd used my own ground-plan. Later came the era of the coloured cords, and traversing the maze became a deceptively simple business. Now that the cords had been removed I was as liable to get lost as the stupidest workman. If I'd known what was going to happen I'd have taken the trouble to memorize the plan, difficult though it would have been. I'd even have had it tattooed on my chest in indelible ink . . .

I reckoned Gabriel would bottle up his curiosity for at least another three or four hours. Finally he wouldn't be able to resist any longer the urge to snap on the light and see what was happening to us. So we had that much of a start.

If you want to get out of a maze, nine times out of ten you can do it by keeping your hand glued to one wall or the other. You'll go down one blind-alley after the other, but if you stick to the same wall it will take you out of the blind-alley and lead you forward again. You'll cover ten times the ground you need to cover. You'll grow dizzy from doubling back. But in the end you'll reach your goal. Of course, if the maze has a fancy ground-plan with galleries that steer you back into the galleries you've already traversed, the system won't work. Like Gabriel's rats, you'll go round and round in small circles until you collapse from exhaustion. I'd designed the El Pardo Maze in such a way that the going would be relatively simple until the half-way mark. There were no blind alleys in the first half to channel the victim back to his starting-point and make him feel as if he'd fallen down a ladder in snakes-and-ladders. Gabriel and I had jointly decided that we wouldn't start trying to break down our victim until he'd reached the half-way point. We'd encourage him to think the maze was child's-play. The first thirty minutes were easy. Up till then the design was straightforward. Then, just when his mood was gay, his spirits were high, he was complimenting himself on his cleverness and looking forward to his dry martini—it was then his troubles really started . . .

I struck out purposefully. My knuckles caressed the smooth cold surface of the wall. The corridors were wide and of uniform width. There were no obstructions. There was no difficulty in walking down them in the dark. The only snag was that when I reached the end of one corridor and turned to enter the next one I tended to do so too abruptly. Astrid, moving straight ahead, was brought up with a violent jolt that jarred us both. After a few minutes I learned to keep my left arm well extended and slow down as soon as I felt my knuckles leave the wall and encounter empty air.

I kept asking: '*Are you all right? . . .*' And her whisper would come back to me out of the darkness a step ahead or a step behind me: '*Yes! . . . Yes! . . . I'm all right!*'

After a while I lost track of time. I plodded along like an automaton, mechanically registering the termination of one wall and the start of the next. My head seemed to be growing lighter. My brain was swelling and turning mushy. I couldn't gauge size or distance. At one moment my feet seemed six inches away and the next moment they were six yards away. The darkness was churning and boiling. Either it was expanding and rushing away from me or else it was shrinking and smothering me. I marched along in a daze. I knew my mind was liable to slide back into its former dream state yet was unable to do anything to stop it. How far did we walk, winding in and out, backwards and forwards, left and right, up one ramp and down another? My head was still throbbing from Gabriel's knock-out drops. My eyes were smarting and watering. My mouth was dry. My stomach was complaining. My shin bones were so sharp and sore I felt they'd cut through the skin. The maze was so large we'd planned to set up tables at intervals with drinks and food. Needless to say, they hadn't been set up for *us* ...

My right hand was beginning to ache from gripping Astrid's wrist. I was glad Gabriel hadn't turned on that lunatic music again. He ought to have done: it would have made a great contribution to our misery. As it was, the darkness seemed to be roaring all around me. Now it muttered, now it threatened to burst my eardrums, like a tempest in a forest tearing at the leaves and snapping the tops of the boughs. Sealed in that blackness all kinds of fantastic images reared up in front of me ... Gabriel's white bull ... his mother's proud white face ... Astrid's silver negligée ... crimson jets of blood spouting from a severed neck ... horses wheeling and winding in an intricate chain ... locomotive falling off a high wooden trestle ... shuffling on my knees round and round and round the pavement of a church ... burning thatch hissing and crackling in my ears ... black sack over my head as I drop drop drop drop drop drop drop drop through a trap-door ...

What kept my feet moving in a slogging rhythm was hatred. I pushed the other images aside so I could concentrate on the image of Gabriel's bobbing, grinning, moist-lipped face as he mouthed and gesticulated his way through one of his monologues. He'd thrown us into his maze and slammed the bolt as if we'd been marionettes boxed up in one of his peepshows. He was putting us through our paces in the way he put his toy trains through their paces upstairs. I hadn't realized what a drive he'd got to act God . . .

I was jolted out of this catatonic mood by what was to be the most demoralizing incident to happen so far. I don't know how to explain it or whether any explanation is possible. I only know that at some point a kind of low rumbling had begun. I can't tell you exactly when. It was one of those sounds that seems to have started a very long way off and a very long time ago. It resembled the noise emitted by the thirty-two-foot stop of a giant organ. The sound takes the form not so much of a noise as of a sub-terranean shaking. You detect it not with your ears but in the pit of your stomach. It was as if some great black pulse had started to beat in the darkness. It was like the first dim stirring of an earthquake. Some words popped into my mind. '*A terrifying sound . . . like thunder . . . and the Great Labyrinth is plunged in perpetual darkness . . .*'

The noise grew and grew. It mounted and mounted until it became a shattering roar. I thought the top of my head would come off. If I'd been able to identify what it was I probably wouldn't have been so appalled by it. It sounded like a gigantic beast in agony. They say the word *panic* comes from the mind-bursting dread which men and women experience when they hear the unearthly bellow of the god Pan in the depths of the forest. Panic like that was what I felt. I was hearing the sound of fear itself—the elemental fear that plucks at the root of the

brain. In the primeval blackness some shaggy monstrosity was clambering out of its hatch. It was the cry of
the Minotaur, the cry you sometimes hear in the bullring
when the bull stands on the crimson sand with its muscles
shredded and lungs punctured and slavering grey tongue
lolling out. An unseen shape was breathing its foul breath
on me in the blackness. My spine had locked and my legs
had turned to water. The cry was magnified to freakish
proportions. Was it simply an amplified screech transmitted by the loudspeakers? Was Gabriel trying an
acoustical experiment on us? Or had he accidentally
tripped one of the switches on the control-panel and
filled the maze with a mechanical scream? Or was it the
voice of Gabriel himself? Whimpering with the weight
of his rage and pain? . . .

The shout had brought me to a halt. When I recovered my faculties I found I was running. Running
hard.

The unthinkable had happened. The worst thing
of all.

Astrid and I had become separated. I was no longer
grasping her wrist.

Black.

Somewhere in the past few distracted moments we'd
lost touch.

Black black black.

Where was she?

Black black black black black black black.

Then I heard her screaming.

BLACK.

Screaming my name.

BLACK BLACK BLACK.
Screaming screaming.
BLACK BLACK BLACK BLACK BLACK BLACK.
'Astrid! . . . Astrid! . . .'

NO alternative now. I had to use the flashlight. I snatched it out of my pocket. The beam splashed a dazzling white oval against the wall ahead of me. Its outline was as sharp as if cut by scissors. When I swung it about it gave me eerie glimpses of myself against the silvered walls. My limbs in their stark black-and-white garb were curiously angular and stick-like.

Switching on the flashlight restored my presence of mind. Rushing about was stupid. It would lead me deeper into the maze in the wrong direction.

I stopped and shone the beam on one end of the corridor then the other. If she was in a neighbouring corridor she'd see the beam and follow it. I advanced up the corridor to the next bend and went on playing the beam on this side and that. I kept on calling her name. I didn't whisper now. I shouted.

God knows where she'd got to. A minute or two was more than enough for us to get parted irretrievably. I blamed myself for my carelessness.

Paradoxically, it was Gabriel who intervened to save us. He must have been sitting there in the control-room with his glass of milk in his hand. He must have caught sight of a flicker of light on the control-panel. It would have told him we had a flashlight. And if we had that, what else might we have? The position of the spark of light on the screen would also warn him that instead of zigzagging about in an aimless fashion we were meeting the challenge of the maze in a purposeful way. He would have decided to switch on the lights again so he could check on us by means of the scanners.

The bright glow grew more rapidly, as if he was turning up the lights in a hurry. My eyes began to tingle. I blundered into walls and went on shouting her name.

I was lucky. I don't know if the maze had led her round in a circle or whether she'd retraced her steps: but all at once I heard her calling out. I started to move in what I judged was the direction of her voice. For several ghastly minutes we appeared to be stumbling down corridors which were parallel yet inaccessible to each other. We could hear one another but couldn't make contact. The pall of nightmare dropped over me again.

Then suddenly through the watery haze that was pricking my eyes I saw her run across the top of the corridor I was in. If Gabriel hadn't switched on the lights I'd have missed her. Our naked feet were soundless in the pile of the carpet. I uttered a cry and broke into a run. My head was buzzing and my thighs and shins made me feel as if I'd been put on the rack, but I managed to reach the corner with a fair turn of speed. Facing me was a dividing corridor with three branches. My heart sank.

I went to each of the branches in turn. When I shouted her name I realized my voice was growing hoarse and feeble.

Then—eyes blazing and hair flying—she came springing out of the middle corridor and bounded into my arms.

And at practically the same instant the damned racket

started up again. Not the fatuous music — the bull-roaring, or whatever it was. Once again it began as nothing more than a low-pitched reverberation and soared by degrees to an all-embracing, oceanic scream. It was enough to melt the flesh on your bones.

We clung to each other as if it was a hurricane that was going to blow us away. She lifted her shaking hands and pressed them to her ears. She was reaching the end of her tether. I didn't know where I'd find the resources to hang on much longer myself.

There is something restorative about hatred. It makes the adrenalin flow. I jerked my head like a snake this way and that in fury. If Gabriel was watching us he'd have seen the venomous expression on my face.

I was convinced he *was* watching. He was spying on us as he'd spied on us in Los Angeles and New York. Getting a kick out of registering the mess we were in. I swung my head from side to side as if I expected him to stroll round the corner with the familiar facetious grin on his face.

We were only a yard away from one of the points on the ceiling where the thick glass of a scanner glared down at us in the pitiless light.

All right. I'd give him something to watch. I'd show him I'd got a couple of tricks of my own. He could sit up there puncturing our eardrums and driving us out of our skulls with that atrocious noise. But he'd find he wasn't invulnerable up there in his little box. He'd find out he wasn't God. I'd do something that was like taking a long needle and pushing it slowly right into the pupil of that damned inquisitive eye . . .

I took Astrid, gently forced her to lower her hands from her ears and walked her three or four steps to the right. I positioned her carefully in what I calculated was the best place for her husband to get a good clear look at what we were about to do. I put my hands on her waist and slowly urged her backwards. Her hips came forward and I leaned in towards her and gradually we went down together on to the carpet. I spread her legs and lowered my body between them. I settled myself on my elbows and cradled her head in my hands and began to kiss and caress her with deliberate and ostentatious leisure. I planted long slow kisses on her neck and breasts. I started to make love to her as if we had all the time in the world . . .

She probably thought I'd gone out of my mind. Perhaps Gabriel's madness was infectious. I could never have acted out a vengeful scene like that if I'd been quite sane. There was a submissive and uncomprehending look in her eyes. She murmured some disjointed words that could have been query or protest or endearment.

I put down my head and parted her sweat-sticky hair with my lips and whispered: 'Put your arms round me . . . Kiss me . . . You want me to make love to you . . .'

Her eyes widened. She didn't understand but she could see there was cunning in my madness. She wrapped her arms round me and reached up to fasten her mouth on mine.

I rucked aside the negligée and eased down the bra and nuzzled my lips between her damp breasts. Didn't Gabriel enjoy conducting people to ring-side seats to watch Leonidas going through his paces? I slid my fingers beneath the panties. She quivered, and I felt her knees rise round me and her arms tighten. I began to work the flimsy material away from her buttocks.

The lights went out. All at once. In a rush. No long theatrical fade-out.

I laughed. If this was a battle of nerves, at last I'd won a round. My little scheme had paid off. I'd forced him to switch off the lights again.

I jumped to my feet. I recovered my grip on the flashlight, dangling from its loop on my wrist. I switched it on and helped Astrid up. I felt I hadn't run far enough in finding her to destroy my sense of direction. I was pretty confident I only had to go back one corridor to pick up the original point where I discovered I'd lost her. I reckoned that it couldn't be far now to my first objective, which was situated at roughly the half-way mark.

As I took her hand and started to follow the left-hand wall again, I wasn't really as confident as I kept telling myself I was. What if I'd boobed? What if we were actually walking back towards the entrance? . . . What if Gabriel had succeeded, during one of my absences from El Pardo, in doing something really cunning? Like changing the ground-plan? Or altering the passages so as to open up new blind-alleys? What if he'd managed to change the maze in such a way that now there wasn't any exit? If all the passages were sealed in an endless circle and there wasn't any way out at all? . . .

We were moving along briskly, hugging the wall, when she suddenly said:

'The air-conditioning . . .'

I didn't slow down.

I asked:

'What about it?'

'Why isn't it working?'

We came to a corner and rounded it.

She repeated:

'Why isn't it working?'

'It's working. We're hot. We've been walking too fast.'

'No. It's getting hotter and hotter. Can't you feel it?.

She was right. I could. The air was definitely warmer and heavier.

Another corner.

'Well?' she asked.

'Imagination. Try not to think about it.'

'It's *not* imagination! It's stifling!'

Without stopping, I tried to figure out what was happening. It wasn't difficult. Gabriel had shut off the air-conditioning and pushed the heating up as far as it would go. I could hear the dry hiss of the heated air pumping through the louvers above us. Soon the needle on the regulator on the wall of the control-room would read over a hundred degrees.

My silk shirt was soaked through. I felt the sweat saturating the cloth on the inside of my thighs. Astrid's hand was wet and slippery.

'What are we going to do?' she asked. And then, when I didn't answer: 'Darling! We just can't go on walk-ing!...'

If we stopped, we were beaten. We'd lie down like a pair of exhausted animals and die there. For the first time I felt her offer resistance. She was ready to rebel. She wanted nothing more than to be left alone, to sink down to the floor and welcome whatever it was she'd have to endure.

I pulled her along by force, moaning and protesting. We were gasping for air as if we'd been thrust into a furnace. As we were struggling up what felt like the millionth ramp and turning the millionth corner she collapsed and let herself fall forward without any attempt to save herself. I blundered on a couple of steps and had to go back and heave her up. As I bent I swore at her so violently her white face craned back at me in sheer surprise. I wrenched her up by her arms with a bruising roughness that made her squeal.

Left turn, right turn—right and left—left and right. I hauled her along behind me with an iron resolution. The atmosphere was rapidly becoming so sweltering that to my muddled mind the beam of the flashlight was a bar of white molten metal and the blackness around it was boiling and bubbling.

I'd almost forgotten in that hellish cauldron of a maze what it was I was looking for. Then suddenly . . . mercifully . . . I came upon it. One moment there was just the frightening sameness of one corridor after another. The next—and there was the vivid scarlet bulkhead jutting out of the right-hand wall ahead of me in one of the most interminable-looking of the corridors.

We were on the right track. I'd achieved my first goal. We'd reached the dead-centre of the maze. And my harshness with Astrid in making her hurry was justified: another few minutes (or however time was reckoned down here under the ground) and we'd have been scorched and scalded into oblivion . . .

I released her and let her drop to her knees, then crumple forward on her face. I fumbled the hammer out of my pocket and crossed to the bulkhead. It was five feet across, stretching the whole length of the wall from ceiling to carpet. I started to pound blindly at its scarlet panels, but they didn't splinter fast enough and I knew I was losing energy. I had enough sense to reverse the hammer and use the claw-head to tear at the edge of the bulkhead, where the joints were. I needed more strength than I had left, but actually the panels yielded easily, the screws snapping out of their holes like miniature gunshots. It was lucky the bulkhead casing was only a temporary one, of wood, painted to look like steel for the purpose of the opening party. In a few days time it was scheduled to be replaced with a proper metal one.

When I'd stripped off enough of the covering, I was confronted with a tangle of wires beneath. This was the place where all the wiring of the maze ran through a central core and was available for inspection and repair. Essentially it was a big junction-box. I wasn't an electrical expert and I didn't know what those thickets of wires signified—fat wires like snakes or thin ones like worms, distinguished from each other by plastic sheathing all the colours of the rainbow. I played the flashlight at random, then took the hammer and used the claws to rip at the wires indiscriminately. I'd destroy them all. It was like breaking up the action of a huge piano or a gigantic harp. The treble strings parted easily while the bass strings offered more resistance. When Astrid came crawling up on her hands and knees to watch me I slapped the flashlight into her hand and ordered her to hold it on the bulkhead as I worked. I needed both of my hands for some of the thicker wires. There were streams and cascades of blue and white sparks like a flurry of Chinese fire. I could feel the furry electrical kick in my wrists in spite of the solid insulation of the handle. I'd got to get the job done somehow, kicks or no kicks. It was our only chance to cut off the heating, which otherwise was going to kill us. I'd also be cutting off the air supply—but I had to take a chance on that. I hoped there'd be enough air to last our remaining time in the maze. And by stopping the fans and the air from circulating I could prevent Gabriel blowing any kind of toxic material through the air-vents and getting us that way. I'd dealt with the lights and the television-screen as well. When the wires were smashed he couldn't see us or keep track of us. I'd have gained us a certain amount of new room to manoeuvre.

Naturally, when he discovered I'd smashed the electrical system he wasn't going to simply go on sitting still up there. It would madden him even more. I was stoking up his fury. He'd hit back. How, I didn't know. But he'd slash back at us, we could be sure of that.

I'd face that when it came. Meanwhile, I had to work out a plan for threading our way through the second half of the El Pardo Maze.

Think. Think. Think. Think. Think. Think. Think.

I was deadly tired, and needed a rest.

The time had come for what orchestral conductors call a Ruhepunkt, a breathing-space. God knows what hurdles lay ahead. It was dangerous to loiter—but equally dangerous for us to plod on without enough strength to lift our arms over our heads.

I lowered my body to the floor beside Astrid and relieved her of the torch. My limbs felt as clumsy as if they were encased in an old-fashioned diving-suit. I could feel small muscles quivering in my calves, in the upper part of my arms and inside my thighs. Astrid, still on her hands and knees, came close to me where I lay sprawled with my legs out against the wall and laid her head on my knee. I switched off the flashlight. The sudden tremendous darkness was soothing and healing. The air didn't seem so baking hot. Already it seemed to be a few degrees cooler. I closed my eyes and let my limbs go slack—and immediately started to float off into sleep . . . brown leaves drifting outside the white lace curtains . . . red sportscar with skis strapped on the roof . . . sapphire sapphire sapphire sapphire . . .

I had to expend a colossal amount of will-power before I could force myself to open my eyes. I compelled myself to switch on the flashlight. My eyelids seemed to be gummed together and lead weights were attached to them. To prevent myself dozing off I started to check in a bleary way through my pockets. Screwdrivers . . . duster . . . key . . .

A chill sliced through me.

Key?

No key.

No key! . . .

My weariness ebbed in a flash. I leaped to my feet. Astrid's head dropped on the floor. She came awake with a little moan. In a fever I took everything from my pockets and let them clatter to the ground. I thrust my fingers into every crevice in search of that key.

NO KEY!

Oh my God, I must have dropped the bloody thing. A mile back? Two miles? Three miles? Four miles? At the entrance? How could I face trudging back to where I'd started from, this time keeping my hand on the right-hand wall, sweeping every foot of the floor with the flashlight?

Up till now I'd been trying hard to keep any hint of my inner terror and despair from communicating itself to Astrid. Now I groaned aloud.

The beam of the flashlight, circling idly, struck the red side of the wrecked bulkhead. I took a step towards it and savagely scuffed at the bits of torn wood with my bare foot. It was nothing more than a baffled reflex. The beam happened to tilt downwards and as I kicked at a shattered plank of plywood something bright gleamed up at me.

The key!

You can imagine how avidly I pounced on it and the care with which I put it back in my pocket. It must have fallen out when I was battering at the bulkhead.

As I stood there with relief washing through me I heard a little whimpering sound. I thought it was me—then realized it was Astrid. I went back, got down beside her and spent the next few minutes comforting her as one comforts a child.

She grew calmer, but I realized we simply had to rest a little while longer no matter what fiend was at our heels. We had to. And I wanted to try and work out what to do if we got as far as having a chance to use the key. Gabriel wasn't just going to let us stroll calmly out of the maze and walk away . . .

What I did next couldn't have been much more reassuring to Astrid than any of the things I'd done before.

As I sat there, with her crouching against me, I unbuttoned my shirt and pulled it off. I propped the flashlight against the upper part of my leg and started to tear the damp silk into strips. As I worked my brain was furiously shaping the next part of my campaign.

She lifted her head and stared at what I was doing. The beam of light struck up under her chin, throwing a shadow across her face so it seemed to be cut in half. Her tired eyes glittered at me out of deep pools of darkness. I tore off a piece of the shirt and handed it to her, indicating that she should copy me. Giving her something to do might take her mind off her troubles. Fortunately, the shirt tore easily.

I shredded the silk into strips about an inch and a half wide. Then I took each strip and tore it into individual pieces about three inches long. You can get a surprisingly large number of pieces of that size from an evening shirt, size forty—and we were going to need every single one of them. We put the pieces on the floor between us, and the pile grew to quite respectable proportions. We ripped up even the cuffs and the collar, and I saved the buttons and put them carefully in my pocket. This was a situation in which anything, however trivial, might sooner or later come in useful. It was almost pleasant, sitting there performing that bizarre little ritual. I could feel the air on my naked torso. The temperature was definitely dropping. The only thing that spoiled our little interlude were certain small matters such as hunger, thirst, and fear.

'Astrid.'

'Yes?'

'We'll have finished this job in a moment. We'll have to be moving on . . .'

'Oh . . . yes! . . .'

'I'll be using the flashlight, so there's not much danger we'll get separated . . .'

She uttered a small anxious sigh. I patted her hand.

'If it happens, though, we've got to handle it differently from last time . . .'

Another nervous sigh.

'If you find you're lost, stop where you are and sit down and don't do anything. Understand? Don't move. Wait where you are. Let *me* find *you*. Understand?'

I was stuffing the mound of rags in my left-hand pocket, with the hammer and the other tools. There wasn't room for more than a quarter of them, but I wasn't going to clutter up the pocket where I'd put the key. I wouldn't make *that* mistake again . . .

I told her: 'Take the rest of the rags and carry them carefully. Don't drop any. Dropping them could confuse us—lead us the wrong way.'

'What are we going to do with them?'

'You'll see.'

She got to her feet and made a container of her arms. I loaded the rest of the rags into them.

'Listen,' I said. 'We've got the most complicated section of the maze ahead of us. It's going to be pretty wearing—but if we could tackle the first part, we can steer our way through the rest of it. We're going to use these rags as markers. We couldn't do that before, as we wouldn't have had enough for the whole maze, and anyway it wasn't strictly necessary in the first half.'

'I don't see . . .'

'Trust me.'

'But Gabriel . . .'

'Don't think about him. Just concentrate on the job in hand. Take every minute as it comes. Don't think further ahead than that.'

'I . . . I'll try . . .'

'Good girl. Ready?'

'I . . . think so . . .'

'Right—here we go!'

The fact that we were on the last lap—even if it was likely to be a long one—added a certain amount of spring to our step. It was also encouraging to be acting according to a definite plan, even if I hadn't any idea how well the plan was going to work out.

What I did was this. We walked down the middle of each passage following the circle made on the floor by the flashlight. Whenever we came to the end of a corridor, where it split into two or three branches, we took the left-hand branch. In the original plan the point where a corridor branched off into other corridors was called a *node*—a technical word derived from the French *noeud*, a knot. It was a term used by Gabriel's rat-fancier from the University of New Mexico, so we borrowed it. At each node I placed at the entrance of our chosen branch three of our little strips of rag. We went on, and I made certain we kept up a businesslike pace. I wanted to work up a purposeful rhythm for this final act of the drama.

None the less, it seemed an age before I once more encountered one of the nodes where I'd previously put three of my rags. There were moments when I had a sickening feeling we'd somehow got out of the second half of the maze and regressed into the first half. That would have been our death-sentence.

When I saw those three strips shining again in the beam I shook with joy. Literally shook. I took a single piece of rag out of my pocket and put it at the end of the passage we'd just left. This was a node with three branches, so I selected one of the two other passages, unmarked by the sign, and we entered it.

That was my strategy. We'd keep on walking until we came to a two- or three-branched node, and if there were no unmarked paths at that point it meant we'd already explored this particular branch-system. In that case we'd turn round and retire down the corridor by which we'd arrived. However, if we reached a node with one or more unmarked paths leading from it, we chose one of them and as we entered I stopped and marked it with two strips of rag.

In this way we could be certain we were visiting every part of what remained of the maze. We made it a rule when we reached a node never to take a three-marked path unless there were no paths unmarked or with one mark only. And when we entered a one-mark path, we added the two marks we always left on leaving a node. Thus it became a three-mark path at that node.

Astrid didn't understand what was going on and I hadn't got time or breath to explain it to her. But as we began to run across more and more of the silk strips she realized I was fathoming out the right way to go. Her attitude became intent and her steps grew alert. She was ready with a handful of rags the instant I needed them. Of course, this was a tedious method of solving the problem but at least it was sure and bound to be shorter than the primitive hand-against-the-wall method I'd used before. But my supply of rags was limited and I began to worry about running out. I'd long ago emptied my pockets and Astrid's pile was getting low. Still, there was always my trousers and Astrid's negligée.

However, on the whole I felt better than I had for several hours. Cautiously, tentatively, I allowed myself a tiny glow of optimism. There was no doubt the air was cooler—even slightly chilly? But the new atmosphere made me feel fresher and more vigorous. I don't want to give the impression we'd somehow got used to the maze, or that the horror and creepiness were in any way wearing off. But I was certainly feeling a good deal more confident.

I was just telling myself that those ramps, leading unendingly up and down, were the worst part of it—and cursing myself for my own ingenuity in putting them there—when . . .

'*Listen!*'

Astrid stopped. I stopped too.

'What?'

'Can't you hear it?'

'Hear what?'

'That noise? . . .'

I listened. I shook my head. 'No.'

'You can't?'

I tried again. Nothing. 'Come on,' I said, 'we've got to . . .'

'*Wait!*'

To humour her, I listened one last time.

She asked: 'Hear it?'

Yes. Now I heard it. Voices. She shrank back against the wall, clutching what was left of the rags. I gave her shoulder a squeeze, took the rags and pushed as many as I could in my pocket, keeping the rest in my free hand.

'Come on!'

We set off again. I didn't want to loiter, brooding about the presence of other people in the maze. Why would they be there if they weren't stalking us? . . .

Gabriel must have known we hadn't collapsed. He'd decided to track us down. Perhaps I'd set him off by the way I'd made love to Astrid. Perhaps he wanted to cut the comedy short. Short and sharp.

We couldn't be far away from the exit. The El Pardo Maze was big — who knew that better than I? — but it had to come to an end somewhere. The rear entrance was formidable. It had a door almost as solid as the door of the vault. But I had the key. I'd ordered that rear door myself and driven down to inspect it at the foundry at Texarkana. It was shipped to El Pardo provided with four sets of keys. I'd handed Gabriel three and kept back one for myself. It had been useful to have it while I was still working on the maze. It was this one that I'd slipped off my key-ring — acting on the merest hunch — and put in my emergency bundle under the step.

I knew that getting through that rear door was going

to take more than just a twist of a key. I thrust the thought away from me. At the moment I wasn't going to set myself a bigger goal than just reaching the exit.

Actually, if Gabriel and his companion (the faithful Larry?) were in the maze, why shouldn't we stand a fairly good chance of getting out ahead of them? Why shouldn't we leave them floundering about in the corridors, miles behind us? . . .

I put on a spurt. Practically all the branches at the nodes had marks on them now. Another few turns — another few minutes — *had* to bring us to the exit.

I kept listening for voices. Why had someone called out in the first place? Did they break silence because they had the same difficulty as we did in trekking through the maze? Encouraging. Gabriel couldn't be using my original sketch-plan. It was too big. Of course, he'd had time to make a photographic reduction or trace a route from the master-panel in the control-room. All the same, without light, traversing the maze was bound to be confusing.

It was cold. The temperature had dropped further and quicker than I'd expected. We'd started to shiver: but at the same time the silly idea got stuck in my mind that the cold air was coming in from the outside and we must be close to the exit.

I don't know what it was that revealed the fact that we were really and truly approaching the end of the maze. It could have been just animal instinct — the nocturnal creature sensing the dawn before the stain of light appears on the horizon. I recall that for some time I'd been haunted by a dread that my flashlight batteries were running down and the beam was getting weaker. I had the same sensation you sometimes get on those endless Texas highways when you glance at the petrol-gauge and see your tank is nearly empty. You can almost feel the petrol draining away and wonder if you're going to make it to the next petrol-station. I had that same feeling about the flickering beam ahead of me. I was sure it was growing feebler and paler by the second. It became an obsession. I strained my eyes at the yellow circle and tried desperately to persuade myself it was as bright as ever . . .

And then a possible, a marvellous explanation crept into my tired brain. Perhaps the beam of the flashlight *was* growing weaker . . . because the surrounding darkness *was growing lighter! . . . Light was seeping in from the world above! . . .*

I started to run, even though we were at the bottom of a ramp and had to run uphill. I could hear Astrid panting behind me.

We had only to keep running towards the light. We must be in the last corridor.

I was sprinting now, desperate to reach the end of the long steel alley-way, when . . .

BAM!

Something struck the wall at shoulder-level like a blow on an anvil and went shrilling away down the corridor ahead of us. I knew immediately what it was: but the shock was so intense I couldn't help freezing in my tracks and looking round.

A mistake.

Another explosion set the air in the corridor vibrating

and there was an almost simultaneous clang as the bullet hit the wall at the far end.

I fled. I could hear Astrid's breath whistling in her throat as she fled at my side. There wasn't another shot and we managed to scramble into the mouth of the corridor on our left, the side nearest us.

It was a miracle I hadn't fallen and smashed the flashlight. I didn't even remember how between the first and second shots I'd somehow had the presence of mind to switch it off. All I'd seen reflected in the steel walls was a wide flare of light like the light from a powerful electric lantern. Somewhere in that pool of light stood Gabriel, a hunting-rifle hugged into his shoulder, Larry beside him.

I switched on the flashlight for a second, keeping the beam turned away from the corridor we'd just left. I saw Astrid jammed back against the steel wall as if she wanted to melt through the metal, her breath bursting out of her as if she'd never be able to get it back.

'You all right?'

A stupid question: but she still had enough courage and presence of mind to give me a little wobbly nod. I took her hand and pressed it hard, then raised it to my lips and kissed it. I swung the beam of the flashlight round carefully and shone it on the floor. We'd taken refuge in the left-hand corridor of a node. There were two strips at the entrance, a yard from my bare foot. The strips told me we'd already traversed this particular corridor. Another flick of the torch told me that the corridor directly across the way from this one was unmarked by rags, and that that was the one we should have taken—

would have taken, if it hadn't been for the shots. To reach it, we had to cross the corridor we'd just left—the corridor where Gabriel was installed with his rifle, as if this was the deer-hunting season and he was after more heads for his trophy-room, or operating one of the shooting-games in his penny-arcade, or practising in his private shooting-gallery . . .

I had to act quickly. He'd come stealing silently down that corridor at any moment. He'd flush us out where we stood cringing together and blow off our heads without further ado. He must have gone crazy to throw all his former plans out of the window like this. He'd arranged for us to die of terror, exhaustion, thirst, starvation—deaths he could have brought about simply by closing an iron door and getting in his car and driving away. Our deaths could never have been traced back to him. Now, when he shot us, there'd be personal involvement, a big mess to clean up, bodies to be disposed of. I suppose he now thought a gradual death was too good for us and wanted the satisfaction of finishing us off with his own hand.

Why the delay? What was keeping him? Why wasn't he already standing there facing us, gun in hand? Perhaps even in his madness he still retained a spark of prudence. If I'd managed to wreck the central nerve-centre of the maze I could still be dangerous. He may have figured that since I'd got a flashlight and other implements there was more than a logical chance I'd got a gun as well. In Texas, that was a reasonable inference.

I reckoned he'd either try to intercept us or get ahead of us. Since he'd come this far so quickly he'd certainly got a map. But I was sure there was a definite glimmer of light in the square outline of the corridor we had to enter. We were near the exit. We had to move before Gabriel stepped in to block us off.

I judged the angle of the path we'd have to take and switched off the flashlight.

I took Astrid's hand again and whispered: 'We're going to run across this next corridor into the corridor beyond. He can't shoot in the dark . . . Ready?'

Without waiting for a reply I darted across the corridor, pulling her after me. I'd taken three steps when there was a savage detonation. Astrid screamed. Her knees buckled. My forearm slammed against a wall in the blackness as I hauled her to safety.

Gabriel *could* shoot in the dark. He had an infra-red gunsight.

He'd hit Astrid. So much for the assumption that whatever he'd got in mind for me he'd only put her in the maze to teach her a lesson. He was going to kill her. My forearm was almost numb. I switched on the flashlight and examined her as she kneeled leaning forward against my knees. The bullet had creased her back, ripping the negligée and nicking the strap of her bra. There was a shallow runnel in the flesh from which the blood was oozing.

I picked her up in my arms and carried her further along the corridor in the dark, her legs bumping against the wall. She was unconscious or paralysed with fear. She couldn't have started feeling the effect of the bullet yet.

At the end of the corridor I felt the cold wall come to

an end. I used the flashlight again. Same situation. The unmarked branch of the node was ahead and could only be reached by crossing another corridor. I floundered forward, expecting a bullet in the ear or the side of my neck.

A shot screamed past. I dodged back. Where had it come from — behind me or the corridor on the right? If he was behind me I was a dead duck. There was no avoiding it: I had to make certain.

I took one of the two screwdrivers out of my pocket and awkwardly, hampered by Astrid's dead weight, tossed it out across the lateral corridor. It hit the wall on the far side with a sharp clatter. Instantly a shot scraped sparks from the steel wall as if the screwdriver had been a clay-pigeon sprung from a trap.

I gasped at the brutal smack of the bullet: but at least I knew for sure where Gabriel was. Mercifully, he hadn't got behind us. He was tracking us along a parallel corridor and moving ahead to station himself for each shot as we emerged from each of the lateral passageways. He was evidently taking care not to expose himself in case I had that gun. Or perhaps he was merely enjoying himself. I judged he was between twenty-five to thirty-five yards away.

I didn't know how many more lateral corridors we had to cross before we reached the exit. I didn't know how many more ramps we had to climb and descend. There was no doubt now I could detect light in this part of the maze, but it wasn't yet strong enough for Gabriel to see us with the naked eye or for Astrid and me to give up using the torch.

I waited. Gabriel waited. He was probably steadier now, fighting down his rage, settling himself comfortably for the next shot. His hand would be firmer and his eye keener. He'd certainly hit on an excellent way of narrowing the margin between us. A hunting-rifle is a great reducer of the odds . . .

I leaned against the wall to lessen Astrid's weight. I couldn't carry her far in my present state. Her flesh was cold as a corpse's. To my surprise, I wasn't afraid. I wasn't afraid because I'd used up all my fear. I was filled with a weary sulky anger that we'd come so far only to be cut down within sight of the finishing-line. I tried to think what to do next but the thoughts were fused together in my head like frozen ice cubes.

Have you ever heard of *Kukushka* or *Little Cuckoo*? It's a game the officers of the old Russian Army used to play to while away the winter nights in Siberia. The candles in the mess would be extinguished, the curtains drawn tight, the room plunged in darkness. An officer would place himself on a chair against the far wall, facing the door, pistol in hand. The other officers would leave the room and take turns to enter it. The man who entered could enter however he liked — upright, crouching, on his hands and knees, crawling on his belly. He could walk or he could run. He could leap to the right or to the left. The only requirement was that at the moment he crossed the threshold he had to shout: '*Kukushka!*' And as he shouted it, the man with the pistol fired. He fired at where he thought the voice was coming from. So it paid to be quick and to be crafty and to be a ventriloquist.

If I'd been on my own I'd have made a dash for it, or

gone on my hands and knees, or run across stooping like someone playing *Kukushka*. But I'd got Astrid to take care of. I lowered her to the carpet and crept back as silently as I could to the corridor I'd just left. I calculated Gabriel would have gone on ahead to his next position. He wouldn't expect me to retrace my steps. I didn't switch on the flashlight. I crawled out into the lateral corridor and groped around gently at the base of the near wall until my hand closed on the screwdriver I'd thrown a couple of minutes before. I thought Gabriel might just fall for the same trick twice.

I returned to Astrid, picked her up and balanced her on my shoulder as well as I could. I lobbed the screwdriver far down the corridor against the opposite wall. I waited a tenth of a second after the shot went screeching past my hiding-place and made a rush for the opposite corridor. A second shot hit the carpet with a dull smack at what seemed an inch from my heel.

This time I didn't need to use the torch to check the marks in the branches of the nodes. The slight radiance in one of the entrances was unmistakable. I wondered whether it was daybreak outside and whether I hadn't noticed the light sooner because it had been night during our time in the maze. All I had to do was keep going straight ahead. I didn't bother to retrieve the screwdriver. I'd pitched it too close to where Gabriel might be standing, and anyway it was useless to try the trick a third time. I considered using the hammer: it would make a more impressive clang as it struck the steel wall. But Gabriel mightn't fall for it and I'd also be wasting one of my precious bits of hardware. It was only the knowledge that I'd got something to defend myself with that dissuaded Gabriel and whoever was with him from making a direct frontal assault. They knew I'd fight like a cornered animal because I'd got nothing to lose.

I was still fingering the hammer when I remembered the buttons of the silk shirt I'd sacrificed. Awkwardly, shifting Astrid's unconscious body about, hearing some part of her anatomy thump against the wall, I fished the six tiny buttons out of my pocket.

I threw them across the lateral corridor. No answering sound – or none that I could catch. Perhaps they were too light to carry to the far wall. I'd failed to provoke Gabriel into firing prematurely. And I'd run out of objects to throw. It was stalemate – with the odds on Gabriel. I had to move – but when I moved, he'd shoot me. Then I thought of the sapphire ring. It took me what seemed an age to locate Astrid's hand, then her finger. It seemed to take even longer to slide the ring off the finger, even though the sweat on the skin helped me. I gripped it tight and threw it as hard as I could. This time there was a distinct sharp click. It was faint, but I knew that if I heard it then Gabriel would catch it too. Like mine, his nerves were stretched and keyed up to register the slightest noise.

I waited.

He didn't fire.

What was he up to?

I caught a snatch of subdued conversation. Just a few words, but enough to identify Gabriel's quick light voice. A glow rippled along the steel walls of the lateral corridor ahead. He must have told Larry to switch the lantern on. The glow lasted only six or seven seconds then disappeared as abruptly as it appeared. Probably Gabriel thought he might catch me in the open, tiptoeing across the top of the corridor, a perfect target. Or perhaps he'd discovered the light was too garish and problematical and it was better to rely on the infra-red sight. He must have motioned Larry to turn it off again.

I acted with commendable speed and presence of mind. At almost the same second as the light went out I hobbled rather than ran across the lateral passage. The shot Gabriel loosed off ploughed harmlessly into the carpet and was so late and inaccurate he must have pulled the trigger at random.

Once more I was in a position of temporary safety. My strength was definitely on the ebb. He'd also be starting to guess that, whatever else I had, I hadn't got a gun. I couldn't carry Astrid much farther and she showed no sign of returning to consciousness. Here I was, staggering along the corridor and up a steep ramp with Astrid while my adversary was padding along the parallel corridor encumbered with nothing more burdensome than a rifle and a pocketful of cartridges.

I advanced to the mouth of the next lateral corridor. There I put Astrid down. I knelt painfully and deposited her as gently as I could on the carpeted floor. She was breathing lightly and irregularly. I stayed kneeling for a few moments, dead beat, seeking to recover a little strength. I didn't dare pause too long, haunted as I was by the mental picture of Gabriel appearing in front of us, sighting down his gun-barrel. I was also afraid that if I waited too long I'd never manage to whip my stiff limbs into action again.

I floundered to my feet and wallowed along to the end of the corridor. The slope of the ramp felt as cruel as if I was climbing a mountain. I had enough presence of mind to keep well back from the lip of the tunnel when I reached it so as not to expose myself to the sharpshooter down the corridor to my right. I'd got a definite idea he was shortening the distance each time by walking a few feet further forward. I tried to clear the rising mists from my brain as I peered across the intervening corridor at the next step of the obstacle course. How far did I still have to go? . . . How far? . . .

When I raised my eyes, a colossal surge of excitement raced through me. It was as if I'd put my hand on one of the naked wires in the wrecked bulkhead. Opposite me, as I looked up the ramp, there was only one entrance. And beyond it, vaguely emerging in the cold pearly light of day, was the dark glitter of a flight of steel stairs leading up to the rear exit of the maze. These were steps, not a ramp. They rose steeply and majestically—a final sadistic twist in my design. If Gabriel couldn't put a bullet through me in the shadows of the maze, he'd be able to pick me off at leisure as I toiled up that gleaming staircase . . .

All the same, I felt a flash of irrational hope. I was someone trapped in the depths of a cavern who sees the brightness of the cave-mouth looming ahead of him. The fog in my head evaporated. I was seized by a lunatic impulse to storm straight ahead. I choked it down. Thoughts were rushing without logic and sequence through my mind.

I went back to Astrid, took hold of her by the ankles and dragged her as gently as I could manage a dozen yards back down the corridor. I'd decided to leave her where she was. I could act more freely without her and she'd be less open to danger. It would be easier for me to do whatever I'd got to do and come back and fetch her when it was over — if I was still alive. I knelt down and nudged her body close to the wall until she was actually touching it. I wanted her to be far enough back for there to be a good chance of Gabriel's lantern missing her as he passed by in the other corridor.

Moved by a sudden impulse, I bent forward and kissed her cold mouth. Then I got to my feet and went back to the end of the corridor. I looked at the distant staircase, divided from me by the deadly No Man's Land of the lateral corridor. Fifteen feet under fire.

What was I to do?

I was cleaned out of ideas. I couldn't think of anything remotely original, let alone brilliant.

I suppose I actually loitered there for less than twenty seconds. Then I did the first thing that came into my head.

I ran the gauntlet.

I can't say I burst out of my hiding-place like a quarter-miler kicking off from the blocks. I was stiff with cold and half lame. I had to run uphill. But I came out faster than I ever thought I could. The prospect of being sniped at concentrates a man's mind wonderfully.

I hurled myself forward with my head crushed down into my shoulders and my arms swinging.

The gun seemed to go off a yard from my right ear. It

sounded like a cannon. I thought I'd be lifted clean off my feet by the blast and the impact of the bullet. There was a crash. I spun round, tottering. Something stung my cheek and mouth and the top of my chest. I felt a tearing pain. Another explosion and something hit the back of my skull like a brick. The impetus of the double blow and my initial momentum sent me reeling forward and I went sprawling into the mouth of the tunnel opposite. In the same movement I picked myself up and propelled myself forward like a footballer after a tackle. I rolled and scrambled towards the towering staircase like a cat thrown over a high wall.

Gabriel would be close behind me. He'd come hurrying in for the kill. I got to the bottom of the staircase. It was sharp and sheer as the staircase of an Aztec temple. As I prepared to climb I expected the crack of the next bullet in my spine. I thought I'd already been fatally shot.

With my bare foot on the first icy step I happened to turn my head. There was a recess in the wall at the foot of the stairs. I remembered that there was one on each side. They were mere slots in the wall, three feet wide and four feet deep. They weren't intended for any special purpose, though Gabriel thought he might buy a couple of classical statues to stand in them. They were part of the structure. The design had just worked out that way. Instead of making myself an open target on the stairs I might as well postpone my death for a moment. I might as well get my breath back and die with dignity, on my feet, instead of banging and bumping down a flight of stairs like a sack of potatoes.

With a bound I reached the recess, turned and fell back into it. My legs scarcely supported me. I was like a corpse propped in an upright metal coffin. Shivering, I realized that Gabriel's first shot had hit the torch as it swung loose on my wrist, showering me with splinters of glass and cutting my face and chest. The second shot had creased the back of my scalp. I fingered the hair and there seemed to be a flap of wet flesh hanging loose.

From the corner of my left eye as I stood rammed against the wall I could see the topmost stair and part of the square door with its panes of reinforced glass. I stared at the strengthening daylight like a condemned man. The light splashed down the steps and slashed their rigid geometry with gay and sparkling lines.

A few yards away there came a genteel click as if someone was cocking a gun. The sound of a soft shoefall. I slipped the screwdriver into my left hand.

The barrel that came poking past my hiding-place wasn't, as I'd expected, the barrel of a rifle but the barrel of a pistol. I didn't give myself time to philosophize about it. I jack-knifed out of my iron slot and whacked the extended forearm with my broken flashlight. At the same time I brought the screwdriver upwards with a sharp hard jab.

Larry stepped backwards with a gasp. He held his hands upwards and outwards away from him as if they'd been attached to wires. He'd taken off the black blazer but was still wearing the red turtleneck sweater. The sweater was even redder now in the area of the abdomen where the handle of the screwdriver was sticking out just under the breastbone. The blood was spreading over the woollen cloth as if I'd driven a nail into a bag of ink. His black-rimmed spectacles fell off and the gun went up over his shoulder in a blue arc and bounced along the carpet. His knees bent and he went over backwards. He hit the floor with his shoulders and the back of his head like an acrobat doing a back flip. His legs straightened and his arms came up jerkily and his hands folded themselves in a curiously tender way round the haft of the screwdriver without being able to pull it out.

The last thing he saw was the shadowed figure of a man with a bloodied face and savage eyes, barefooted, naked to the waist, neck and body seamed with welts and scratches. I don't know if his eyes were still open as I swung away from him and made for the stairs. I started to mount them using my hands and feet with the agility of a monkey. I hadn't felt any twinge of guilt or disgust at what I'd done—my time in the maze had reduced me pretty much to the condition of an animal at bay or one of Gabriel's rats. My aching head was craned backwards and my eyes were fastened on the metal door above me. I could already make out the thin slit of the keyhole with the corona of daylight streaming through it.

I hadn't climbed more than four or five steps when there was the rip and kick of a bullet. It struck the metal step immediately ahead of me and tore a jagged white sliver from it that missed my head by a centimetre as it whanged away. I flopped forward on my face and stayed motionless.

A few more steps and I'd have . . . have . . . Well . . . no matter . . . not now . . .

I rolled over on my elbows and Gabriel was below me.

He was wearing a red turtleneck sweater like Larry's. He was lowering the gun. It was a bulky weapon with a sling. Clamped to the top was a telescopic sight that looked too large for it. He let his arms drop and held the gun loosely at his hips. In the gloom behind I could make out Larry's body, lying in the same position as it fell.

He wanted me to sweat before he pulled the trigger.

I didn't care much. It was only like putting an exhausted creature out of its misery. My will to live was guttering down. I watched the neatly-clad executioner raising the rifle to his shoulder again in a way that was almost detached. His movements were measured and precise, as they were when he photographed one of his railroad accidents. He was going to extract the last ounce of satisfaction out of killing me. I could almost hear him deliberating with himself where to put the bullet.

I started to rise to my feet, for no particular reason except that it seemed the only act of minor defiance left to me. The snout of the gun tilted with me. It crossed my sluggish brain that he was going to shoot me right in the face. Then the tip of the barrel was depressed again, and I saw that he was going to let me have it in the belly . . . No . . . lower down . . .

If he'd simply gone ahead and loosed off at my face I don't think I'd have stirred a muscle. I'd have accepted it fatalistically like the bull in the slaughterhouse waiting for the lethal spike behind its ear. But that other thing! . . . He was stupid there. I remember I'd already begun to move when the voice came out of the black corridor behind him.

'*Gabriel!*'

The muzzle was swinging to follow me. My attempt to skip to one side would only have delayed the shot by two seconds. The end would have been the same. The shout altered that.

'GABRIEL!'

Astrid. Who else? She came running forward. The shot that had wounded her had ripped her bra and it was hanging loose. Her breasts jutted from the open negligée. With her sweat-plastered blonde hair standing up and streaming behind her she looked like some distracted Fury or goddess of the Underworld. He should have been prepared for it. He should have noticed I was alone on the staircase and must have left her behind. But he was taken by surprise. He whirled around confused, staring, gun sagging. As soon as he saw who it was he lifted the barrel immediately and squeezed the trigger from a position down around the level of his stomach.

She was only a few feet away. He couldn't have missed —except that at the moment when he spun round I was already catapulting down the four or five steps that divided us. I came down on him an instant before the gun went off. I hit him in the back and the gun sprang into the air to his left and he went diving in the other direction. He collided with the wall as he fell and as he tried to get up I was on him again. I got the hammer in my hand and clouted him twice behind the left ear, once as he was rising and once as he was falling.

I tripped over him and nearly went flailing into the wall myself. I took a heavy dive on to the carpet and just lay there. I remember trying to get up but couldn't make it. I think I blacked out . . .

It didn't seem a second before Astrid was kneeling above me and crying and stroking my face. I woke instantaneously to what seemed exactly the same situation.

She had to help me up. I clung to her as I gazed down briefly at Gabriel, then lurched over to take another look at Larry. I kept hold of her while I pointed down at the pistol. She had to keep me from falling as she saw I wanted her to stoop down and pick it up for me. She put it in my hand with a tremour of revulsion. My fingers were so palsied they were hardly able to grasp it.

She had to help me up the stairs. My legs were bars of water. It took an age to reach the top and several light-years longer before I could fetch the key out of my pocket and put it in the lock.

It needed several efforts to turn the key, even though the mechanism was freshly oiled, and several more to turn the ornate bronze handle and open the door an inch . . .

I shuffled off to the right of the door and motioned her to walk through it. She hesitated. I motioned again. She was so used to obeying me by this time that she slowly dragged back the heavy door and stepped round it into the world outside.

The draught of fresh air that curled round the door was so intoxicating it made me dizzy. I'd meant to stand behind the door but the air got to me and I slid down the wall and sat in a nerveless heap in the corner.

I'd guessed from the outset that Gabriel wouldn't leave the rear exit unguarded. Whoever was on duty there had probably been given orders to shoot. But after all these hours, and probably as much as a day and a night in the open, he'd probably be sleepy and sluggish. He'd have been expecting to see me—not Astrid—and her appearance was bound to puzzle him . . .

I seem to recall voices and a car door slamming. At length there were slow and careful footsteps on the broad gravel apron that had been laid only a couple of days earlier outside the door. They stopped for a measured moment, then came on again. I'd been on the verge of dozing off, probably as a result of that anaesthetizing gush of air. I thumped my kneecap with the barrel of the gun to wake myself up.

He came through the door with a pistol held in front of him, just like Larry a few minutes before. I lifted my head and saw his shadow on the frosted panes above me. I tried to raise my legs a little to brace myself. He entered cautiously and stopped at the top of the staircase, weaving his head about.

I shot him four times, twice at the top of the steps and twice as he started to pitch forward into the empty air. I think I hit him all four times though the last bullet might have missed.

Somehow I hoisted myself up off the floor. Somehow I reached the outside. Somehow I pushed the iron door closed again, locked it, and put the key back in my pocket.

THE birds were singing. My eyes hurt. Was it morning or afternoon? Away in the far distance, across the grassless brown meadow that covered the maze, I could make out as a vague blur the white spread of the house, behind its screen of pine trees.

I stood outside the rear exit with its classical pediment and Corinthian columns—a replica of the pediment and columns on the great house to which it was joined by that tortuous and terrible network of underground passages. I rocked backwards and forwards, out on my feet.

I jerked my scattered wits back to the present at the sound of a car starting up. Dimly I registered that there were two cars parked one behind the other on the new service-road connecting the maze with the distant house. One was biscuit-coloured and the other royal blue. The blue car pulled out and drove away past the car ahead of it with a scur and swish of its wheels. We heard it humming away down the drive in the direction of the main gates. Then the noise of its engine died away and the empty shining day was silent again.

We drove back to the house at ten miles an hour. I was fighting against a great wave of blackness. Astrid sat with her head on the back of her seat. Her face was streaked with grime and her hair matted and tangled. My right hand was smeared with blood where I'd wiped it against the wound on the back of my head. The caked black blood was moistened by the sweat that ran down my bare arm. It came off in a sticky smear on the rim of the steering wheel.

There was no one in the house. Gabriel had arranged it that way. He'd sent away all the household servants and gardeners and the last remaining workmen on the site.

We took a shower to remove the blood and dirt. We didn't talk. We were too numb and weary. What was there to say? I cleaned and dressed Astrid's hurt back as well as I could with materials from Gabriel's medicine cabinet and she put a temporary dressing on the back of my head. Then we changed into fresh clothes.

After a little while I rang the State Police.

Upstairs, in the rooms of the empty mansion, the hands of the clocks circled the vacant dials. The locomotives and freight-cars stood idle on the tracks of the model-railway. The miniature racing-cars waited silently on the starting-grid. The model soldiers were drawn up regiment by regiment waiting to be summoned into battle. The bombers and interceptors were suspended motionless in the air.

In the penny-arcade the rows of pinball-machines gathered dust. The player-pianos and mechanical-organs were dumb. The sticks of the ice-hockey teams were raised in frozen attitudes. The batter's bat was lifted as he waited for a ball that was never pitched. The race-horses galloped down the course without gaining a millimetre. The cats on the rooftops snoozed peacefully without anyone to pot at them. The condemned men waited patiently for their executioners to pull the levers.

The kinetic sculpture in the darkened gallery whirred and clicked with nobody to heed them.

Nobody peered through the pinholes to stare at the peep-shows.

The man and the woman in their white robes ran through the mysterious landscape pursued by the cloud of insects and with the volcano spouting flames behind them.

The steel ball ran endlessly across the tilting plate. The fluted glass rod twirled endlessly round and round and round and round and round and round in the make-believe fountain.